Perfect FOR FANS OF DAVID WALLIAMS

Getting serious ABOUT SILLINESS!

WHAT would you do in charge?

Written and illustrated by Tom McLAUGHLiN- FUNNY BY NAME FUNNY BY nature

To all the amazing NHS staff and
key workers who have kept us safe in
these horrible times.
Thank you.

OXFORD
UNIVERSITY PRESS

Great Clarendon Street, Oxford OX2 6DP
Oxford University Press is a department of the University of Oxford.
It furthers the University's objective of excellence in research, scholarship,
and education by publishing worldwide

Oxford is a registered trade mark of Oxford University Press
in the UK and in certain other countries

Text and illustration © Tom McLaughlin 2020
The moral rights of the author and illustrator have been asserted

Database right Oxford University Press (maker)

First published 2020

British Library Cataloguing in Publication Data

Data available

ISBN: 978-0-19-277367-8

1 3 5 7 9 10 8 6 4 2

Printed in Great Britain
Paper used in the production of this book is a natural,
recyclable product made from wood grown in sustainable forests
The manufacturing process conforms to the environmental
regulations of the country of origin.

THE Accidental... PRIME MINISTER RETURNS

Written and illustrated by

Tom McLaughlin

OXFORD
UNIVERSITY PRESS

WE ARE THE CHAMPIONS

'WHERE IS HE?' Jenkins yelled, looking at his watch. 'IT'S FIVE to NOON!'

'WELL, HE'S NOT IN HIS PRIVATE STUDY!' yelled an assistant.

'OR THE LIBRARY,' another assistant added. 'OR THE GARDEN EITHER.'

Jenkins was about to open his mouth again when he saw Betty, the tea lady, doing her rounds with the tea trolley.

'There, there dear, I'm sure the Prime Minister will turn up.'

'I AM THE PRIME MINISTER'S PERSONAL ASSISTANT AND IF I DON'T FIND HIM NOW THEN THIS COUNTRY IS GOING TO GRIND TO A HALT. THINK ABOUT THAT! THINK ABOUT WHAT WOULD HAPPEN IF AN ENTIRE COUNTRY STOPPED WORKING. IF EVERYTHING YOU HAD EVER KNOWN COLLAPSED IN ON ITSELF LIKE A BROKEN STAR!'

'So you don't want a bun?' Betty asked, nervously.

'THIS IS DOWNING STREET. IT IS THE BEATING HEART OF THE COUNTRY! THE PRIME MINISTER IS NEEDED RIGHT NOW TO LAUNCH OUR NEW GREEN SPACES POLICY— IT'S HIS LEGACY. THERE ARE HUNDREDS OF CAMERAS FROM ALL OVER THE WORLD WAITING FOR HIM. I AM SURROUNDED BY THE BRIGHTEST AND BEST MINDS THAT THIS COUNTRY HAS TO OFFER, AND YET DESPITE THIS BEING THE SAFEST, MOST PROTECTED BUILDING IN THE COUNTRY IT APPEARS THAT WE HAVE MISLAID OUR PRIME MINISTER. SO, BETTY, UNLESS THERE'S SOMETHING

YOU'RE NOT TELLING ME AND JOE PERKINS IS ACTUALLY HIDING IN YOUR TEA POT, OR YOU'VE TURNED HIM INTO A BUN, I DON'T THINK A TEA BREAK IS GOING TO CUT IT! WE NEED OUR LEADER BACK. WE NEED JOE PERKINS!'

'Aw, I need you too, Jenkins.' Joe slid down the banister of the grand staircase and landed perfectly next to Jenkins and Betty. 'What did I miss?'

'Sir, where have you been?' Jenkins asked.

'I was in the bathroom, trying to get my hair to part on the other side. Do you know, I've only ever parted my hair one way all my life, isn't that amazing? So, I decided that I was going to shake things up a bit and try the other side.'

'What?' Jenkins asked, completely baffled.

'Well, I've only ever parted my hair on one side— left to right—you see . . .'

'Yes, I get that. But why?' Jenkins snapped. 'It's quite a busy day, you know. We are about to give a press conference to the world in five . . . four-and-a-half minutes, and we really don't have time to be messing around with hairstyles. You're not even dressed!'

'It's fine,' Joe said, flinging off his dressing gown, to reveal a suit that looked remarkably like a pair of pyjamas. 'Everyone laughed when I invented the Pyjama Suit, but look who's laughing now! Is it a pair of PJs or is it a posh suit? What's the answer, Betty?'

'BOTH!' She smiled.

'BOOM! SHE KNOWS IT,' Joe said.

'We don't have time to bask in the glory of your

pyjama suit,' Jenkins said, sarcastically. 'The press is waiting outside.'

'Before you go Sir, please can you sign this?' a junior assistant yelled, shoving a piece of paper and pen into Joe's hand.

'Wait, what am I signing? It isn't anything evil is it?' Joe asked, suspiciously.

'No, just to finalize the latest transport policy,' the assistant said.

'Oh yes, the flying-bus initiative. How's it going?'

'Up and down.'

'Well, that's good. That's what flying things are supposed to do, isn't it?'

The assistant nodded. 'Oh, and the French president would like to invite you over for dinner, Sir.'

'OK, but this time *he's* buying! Can someone book us a table at Nando's?'

'Yes, Prime Minister.'

'Right . . . let's do this,' Joe said, reaching for the door. It was the most famous door in the country, one that countless Prime Ministers have opened over the years, and one which Joe, a thirteen-year-old boy, was about to open in order to make one of the most important speeches of his life . . .

And then he caught sight of his reflection in the mirror by the door.

'WAIT!' Joe yelled. 'What was I thinking?' He peered at himself, and brushed his hair the other way. 'I should never have messed with my parting. It falls a certain way for a reason, it's like messing with the universe!'

Joe ruffled his hair one more time, before finally opening the door.

The flash of a hundred camera bulbs greeted him. It was like being caught in a ferocious lightning storm. Joe waved and smiled as he walked to the podium, flanked on either side by a group of school children who had been waiting to join him. They were only a year or two younger than the Prime Minister himself. Joe looked around and smiled, making sure his gaze fell on everyone who was there. It was a good way to settle everyone's nerves, he found. For him, this was an ordinary day: cameras, questions, and crowds. For everyone around him, it was an extraordinarily exciting glimpse into the life of the most important person in the country, though privately it also made many of them thank their lucky stars it wasn't them in charge.

Joe turned to the girl standing next to him.

'Hello Alice. Thank you so much for coming up with the idea for this brilliant new initiative,' he said.

'Thank you, your Prime Ministerness,' Alice said, nervously.

'Ha!' Joe laughed. 'I like "Prime Ministerness"! I must use that myself.'

'Sorry,' Alice said, going a little pink and wrinkling her nose to stop her glasses falling off.

'Don't be, I want to thank you for your letter,' Joe said. 'I'm glad you and your classmates wrote to me and came all the way here today. And I'm sure the fact that it meant you all got out of double maths had absolutely nothing to do with it.' He chuckled, and all the children laughed along, too.

'Thank you, Prime Minister. There's this bit of ground at the end of our street, where there used to be an old house, which got torn down because it was old and crumbly, and now there's just a few old bricks on that space. I thought, why not turn it into something? Then I read about you in my history lesson, about how you saved your local park, which is how you ended up becoming the Prime Minister, and I knew you would be able to help.'

'In your history lesson? Wow, that makes me feel old!' Joe laughed. 'Well, of course I can help. I'm going to say a few words now, then we're going to have some photos, and then maybe you can come inside for tea and buns.'

Joe stepped up to the podium. 'Hello everyone. Thank you for coming and a warm welcome from Downing Street. We're here to launch a new project called Green Space, the brainchild of Alice here!' Joe grinned. 'These kids, eh? Coming up with great plans and ideas. They'll be wanting to be Prime Minister next!' The reporters chuckled.

'Alice's idea is that every child should have access to a green space, a park to play in, or plant flowers in, or both. And as you know, I have very strong feelings about keeping parks open. That's how I became Prime Minister in the first place. We need more green space in this world, not less, so we're going to build parks on every street corner up and down the land. It's going to be a big project, but I think we can do it . . .' Joe paused before saying, 'Now, I know you will all have a ton of questions—'

But the reporters were all ignoring Joe, and instead they were all busy checking their phones. 'What's going on?' Joe hissed at Jenkins, who was standing off to the side. Jenkins shrugged, trying to find his own phone. Joe looked back at the crowd of reporters. This time, lots of arms were shooting up.

'Ah, at last a question!' Joe pointed at one reporter waving his arm frantically in the air.

'Jonny Weeks of *The Times*. I wondered if you had a comment about the breaking news?'

'What breaking news?' Joe asked.

'According to reports coming in, you, Joe Perkins, shouldn't actually be the Prime Minister after all. Apparently, there has been a huge mistake.'

'What?' Joe said. 'It sounded like you said . . .'

'You shouldn't be the Prime Minister, after all,'

Jonny Weeks repeated.

'Oh, course I should.' Joe smiled, trying to work out if this was a joke that he somehow wasn't getting.

'So you deny the allegation that you should never have got the job in the first place, Prime Minister, or should I call you just . . . Joe?' the reporter asked.

What's going on? thought Joe. I should be Prime Minister . . . shouldn't I? Joe looked at Jenkins, then back at the reporter, and tried to find some words, any words!

HELP!

'Say that again?' Joe said, going very pale.

'Erm, thank you, ladies and gentlemen,' Jenkins said, stepping in front of Joe. 'That's all the time we have for now. We will be releasing a statement to launch our Green Space initiative, later.'

'Yes, that's right. Time for refreshments!' Joe yelled, as Jenkins ushered him back into No. 10 Downing Street. Or at least Jenkins tried to. The person behind the door obviously wasn't expecting Joe to come back in quite so soon and refused to open the door.

'Hello!' Joe said, banging on the door. 'Coooeeeee!'

'Who is it?' A voice came from behind the door.

'Who is it?! Who do you think it is? It's me, the Prime Minister.' Joe turned back to the cameras and waved, as if everything was under control. 'Just testing the door to see if it's super-strong . . . and the good news is, it is. And security is top notch, too. They don't let just anyone in, you know!'

'Let me in,' Joe hissed through the keyhole.

'Oops, sorry, Sir.' The door swung open and Joe, Jenkins, Alice, and her classmates all fell inside.

'Can someone please tell me what's going on?' Joe asked in a panicky voice.

'WHHHHHHHHHHHHHHHHHHHHHHHHHHH
AHAHHAHAHHAHAHAHHAHAH!'

A blood-curdling shriek interrupted the Prime Minister, as his best friend Ajay landed in a heap by his feet.

'Who's been polishing the fireman's pole?' Ajay said, shaking his head.

Joe shrugged. He'd had a fireman's pole installed at No. 10 because . . . well, if you were Prime Minister and you could do whatever you wanted, you'd probably want a fireman's pole instead of stairs, too. Besides, it was handy in case of emergencies, and today was *definitely* starting to feel like an "emergency" sort of day.

'Crikey,' said Ajay, rubbing the seat of his trousers. 'I've generated quite some heat flying down that thing.' He frowned at Joe. 'I thought we agreed, no polishing the pole. I think my trousers may burst into flames and I really don't need that to happen, not again. Anyway, look . . .' Ajay handed Joe his phone. 'As your multimedia strategist and public relations manager, *this* looks pretty bad.'

'DOUBT CAST AS TO WHETHER JOE PERKINS IS ACTUALLY THE PRIME MINISTER!' Joe read. 'Why are they saying this?'

'It's because of that old nincompoop, Percival T. Duckholm. When he made you sign the document making you Prime Minister, he spelt your name wrong!'

Joe and Ajay looked at each other anxiously, remembering how it had all begun . . .

Two years ago, Joe was just an ordinary kid, before his life changed forever. Joe and Ajay were on the way to see Prime Minister Percival T. Duckholm, who was visiting their school, when they spotted a sign at their local park saying that it was about to be closed down and in its place a huge concrete office block was going up.

'We can't let that happen,' Joe said. 'I'm going to ask the Prime Minister to stop it.'

Later that day, Joe did something pretty brave. He pushed his way to the front of the crowd and told Prime Minister Duckholm that he had to help save the park. Unfortunately, Percival T. Duckholm did not take kindly to being told what to do. Besides, he saw no use in parks. They didn't make anyone any money, so what was the point in them?

Percival had simply laughed in Joe's face. Then he said that as a matter of fact he was going to turn ALL parks into big, shiny tower blocks.

Back then, Joe was a pretty meek sort of kid, someone who just melted into the crowd and didn't like to ruffle any feathers. If anyone ever spoke to him like Percival T. Duckholm did, he usually just took it, kept quiet, and let it go. But this was different. Not only did Joe love the park, but his mum worked there too, as the park ranger.

So, Joe did something he'd never done before— he spoke up. Percival T. Duckholm had lit a fire in him that he couldn't put out and he let the Prime Minister have it. I mean *really* have it! It was like every thought and idea he'd ever had cascaded out of him. He told Percival how politicians like him had let everyone down and how he should be caring for people, not trying to make money from them.

Well, Percival T. Duckholm had *never* been spoken to like that before and he was stunned into silence. But Joe hadn't finished. He went on to tell Percival what he, Joe Perkins, would do if he was

Prime Minister. How he'd fix things, how he'd look after everyone and how, above all else, he would keep all the parks just as they were and maybe open some more. Joe was on a roll!

Joe's speech went viral and was shared in homes all around the world. Who was this kid? people said. Let's give him a go!

Joe immediately became the most famous boy in the world, and this was the last straw for Percival T. Duckholm, who'd had enough of being the most hated Prime Minister of all time anyway, and who had a cunning plan. He invited Joe and Ajay to No. 10 Downing Street. They had just expected to hear that grumpy old Duckholm had given in and decided to keep their park open and they watched with excitement as Percival's pen hovered over a bit of fancy-looking paper.

'He's signing it all off,' Joe had whispered to Ajay. 'He's making it all official!'

But, no. It was in fact the moment of Percival's ultimate revenge. When he scribbled his signature, he was actually resigning as Prime Minister and formally naming his replacement: Joe Perkins. Duckholm tricked Joe into signing the piece of paper. 'Let's see how you like this job, if you think you'd be so good at it!' he said, with a cackle. Joe was flabbergasted, though not as flabbergasted as Duckholm's deputy, Violetta Crump. She'd been after Percival's job for years, and now he'd gone and given it to some snot-faced kid.

Well, not only had Joe made the best of it, he had in fact done a pretty good job over the past couple of years and had grown to love being the Prime Minister.

Joe and Ajay stared at Ajay's phone. It would seem that Percival T. Duckholm had made one vital mistake that day in his office. One fatal error . . .

'HE SPELT MY NAME WRONG!' Joe yelled, reading the rest of the news article. 'POE JERKINS?! POE'S NOT EVEN A WORD, LET ALONE A NAME!'

'Yep, I know,' Ajay said. 'They reckon he might

have accidentally sneezed when he was writing it. Jenkins, maybe you could give him a ring and get him to change it?'

'Not possible, Sir,' said Jenkins. 'Mr Duckholm is no longer with us.'

'Really?' Ajay said, 'you mean . . . ?'

'Yes, he's passed on,' Jenkins confirmed somberly.

'Dead?' Ajay asked.

'Indeed,' Joe nodded.

'Poor guy,' Ajay shrugged. 'I mean, he wasn't my cup of tea, but really, I had no idea.'

'You went to his funeral,' Jenkins said. 'As Mr Duckholm was a former Prime Minister, we all went along.'

'Again, it's not ringing any bells,' Ajay shrugged.

'You made a speech, Ajay,' Joe said.

'They asked me to make a speech?' Ajay scratched his head.

'No, no one asked you to make a speech. You just did it anyway,' Jenkins said.

'Wait, the party with the crab cakes? I remember now. The food was brilliant!'

'Yes, I believe that was what your speech was about,' Jenkins sighed.

'It's all coming back to me now. It was such a brilliant day. Well, apart from all the sadness . . .' Ajay trailed off, looking suddenly uncomfortable.

'Needless to say, that's why Percival can't correct Joe's name,' said Jenkins.

'Does that mean you're not the Prime Minister anymore?' Alice asked. 'What about the Green Space project?'

'No . . . well . . . I don't know. What does this all mean?' Joe asked Jenkins.

'I think it means . . .' Jenkins looked down at his phone and then back up at Joe in astonishment. 'Turn on the big TV!'

Suddenly, everyone sprang into action and a huge TV was wheeled into the grand lobby and switched on.

'Alice, I'm so sorry about this,' Joe said.

'Oh, don't worry, this is the most fun I've had in ages.' She smiled. 'It's like living in an episode of the news!'

'Well, grab a bun and take a seat. I have no idea what's going to happen next!' Joe grinned, nervously.

Jenkins turned on the news, to a live interview with Theodore Flunk. He was the leader of the opposition and the man who always had it in for Joe. He was always making jokes about Joe's height and how young he was—two things that Joe couldn't do anything about. Flunk was a mean bully and Joe didn't care for him one jot.

'BOOOOOO!' Ajay yelled out, 'BOOOO, YOU'RE A BIG POO-POO HEAD!'

Ajay threw a bun like a Frisbee at the TV and it hit the screen right on Flunk's nose before ricocheting off and landing in a plant pot.

'AJAY! We have company!' Joe said, nodding at the school children still hanging out in the lobby.

'Sorry, he just gets my goat,' Ajay said, adding, 'and now I've lost my bun.'

'I would like to call upon the "Prime Minister"' (Theodore Flunk did that annoying thing people do, making air quotes with their fingers), 'to resign. And if Joe refuses to resign then we must have an emergency General Election to let the people decide: will it be me or Joe.' Theodore Flunk looked directly down the camera. 'Let's get our election on!' and then he grabbed the reporter's microphone and threw it up in the air. 'And, *mic drop*!'

'And he has the nerve to call *me* childish?' Joe sighed.

'Oh my word, I just heard the news!' Another door swung open and a woman dressed in a sharp suit walked in. 'Come here and give me a big hug, darling. What can I do to make it all better?'

'Oh hi, Violetta,' Joe rolled his eyes. 'How nice of you to drop by.'

ELECTIONEERING

'Please don't squeeze me too tight, Violetta. I'm full of buns,' Joe said.

'Who else needs a hug? What about you, Jenkins? Or you, Betty? . . . Ajay?'

'Come near me and I will take you down with one swipe,' Ajay said, backing away from Violetta. 'You're forgetting that intensive taekwondo course I did at the community centre during half-term.' He tapped his forehead. 'It's all still in here, you know!'

'Ajay, you need to learn to forgive. Move on, heal, love, and, indeed, hug. So what if, a couple of years ago, I tried to ruin Joe's reputation and take over as leader myself? All that is now in the past,' said Violetta, calmly. 'Would you like some rescue remedy?'

'I can't sniff away my rage, Violetta,' Ajay said. 'You tried to destroy Joe and turn him into a laughing stock. All so that you could win power for yourself.'

'I think you may need help, Ajay. You seem very angry,' Violetta said, serenely.

'Right. That's it, Crump. You and me outside. You've awoken the worrier in me.'

'Warrior,' Joe said, correcting him. 'Also, I hate to intervene in a street brawl, but there are a billion press people outside. It wouldn't do for them to see my best mate and the deputy Prime Minister brawling in the street.'

'So, you'd rather we continued this round the back?' Ajay asked.

'NO!' Joe snapped. 'I have learnt to forgive Violetta Crump, and so should you. It's time to move on. We have more important things to worry about, such as WHAT AM I GOING TO DO'!

Jenkins cleared his throat. 'Sir, I think Theodore

Flunk may well be right. We need to settle this once and for all. He's always maintained that you aren't really a proper Prime Minister because you weren't voted in by the people. If you were to call an election and win, then you'd really . . .'

'Stick it to him?' Ajay asked.

'Well, yes,' Jenkins said.

Joe looked around at the sea of faces, all waiting for him to say something. Should he call an election and risk losing, or change his name by law to Poe Jerkins and argue that the legal document he signed is still binding?

'Can I ask a question?' Alice said.

'Of course,' Joe replied, welcoming a moment's distraction.

'What's an election?' she asked.

'Oh, thank goodness I'm not the only one who's a little fuzzy on this,' Ajay said, sitting down next to Alice and munching on another sticky bun.

'Good question, Alice,' said Joe. 'Well, every few years the public get to decide who they want as their Prime Minister, and the best way to do that is to have a vote.'

'Like for school council?' Alice said.

'Exactly. How many people wanted to be your class councillor?'

'Maybe four or five,' she said. 'They all had different suggestions for how they would run things.'

'And you chose the one whose suggestions you agreed with the most, right?' Joe said.

'Yeah!' she smiled.

'Well, in a General Election, everyone votes for which political party they agree with the most, and the leader of that party gets to be Prime Minister and run the country. Does that help?' Joe asked.

'Yeah, loads,' Ajay said. 'It's cleared up a lot of stuff for me.'

'Me too,' Alice laughed. 'So, you have to win the election. I mean, without you, the Green Space initiative won't happen. You have to call a General Election and you have to win, Joe. I mean, Mr Prime Minister.'

'OK,' said Joe. 'Let's do it!'

'And when will the election take place?' Jenkins asked.

Joe checked his diary. 'Two weeks' time? I've got nothing else on that Thursday.'

'Good for me,' Violetta nodded.

'That doesn't give you very much time to plan your campaign, Joe,' said Jenkins, frowning.

'All I need to do, Jenkins, is just be honest and truthful about what I want to do for this country and the people will make the right choice, I'm sure of it. If the people know what's happened and that I wasn't trying to cheat or pretend to be something I wasn't, I am confident that they will give me a second chance.'

'You're *absolutely* certain?' Jenkins asked.

'Um . . . I think so. Now you're making me nervous, Jenkins.'

'It's just that once you call an election, you can't change your mind. It's not like ordering a pizza.'

'Wait, we're ordering a pizza?' said Ajay. 'I'm in!'

'No one's getting pizza, Ajay,' Joe sighed, before turning back to Jenkins. 'Is there a form I need to fill in to start the election off or something?'

'A form?' Jenkins gasped. 'No, no, Sir. It's more than a form.' He walked over to an old portrait on the wall and pulled it to one side, revealing a giant red button. Jenkins made a fist with his hand and hit the button hard.

Instantly, a deafening siren began to wail, like a warning for a radioactive meltdown. Every light in every room began to flicker and then flashed red, keeping in time with the alarm, and then an electronic voice bellowed, 'GENERAL ELECTION LOCKDOWN!' The oak-panelled walls slid around and were replaced with huge computer screens, TVs, and control panels. The entire room suddenly resembled mission control at NASA.

Joe and Ajay looked at each other. They'd had no idea that any of this was here.

'INITIATING GENERAL ELECTION PROTOCOL!' Jenkins yelled into the Downing Street intercom.

'PROTOCOL INITIATED,' the robotic voice yelled in return.

'Whoa,' said Jenkins, breathlessly. 'I've never had to activate the emergency alert before. I must admit I always thought it was made up when I read about it in the Downing Street manual. A futuristic flight of fancy, as it were. I feel quite modern!'

Joe stood back and took it all in. It felt as though he'd just started a war, not asked people to toddle off down to their local Scout hut and put an 'X' in a box, to cast their vote.

'All this is for an election?' Joe said in shock.

'Yes. Voting is very important,' Jenkins said seriously. 'The power that the government and its Prime Minister have is immense. It's like handing someone the keys to a space rocket. They are in charge of your hospitals, your schools, and all the money you give them through taxes.'

Paul Mifinger

Jenkins paused and beckoned Joe to follow him to the hall staircase, where the portraits of many previous Prime Ministers, going back centuries, hung on the walls.

Lady Dorothy Pinkleton

'Look at them all,' he said quietly, as he climbed the stairs with Joe behind him. 'Men and women of influence, who each for a brief moment in time became captain of the ship that is our great nation, steering it through choppy waters, away from danger and keeping us all safe. You are one of the lucky ones, Sir. You have already steered that ship. But elections are difficult things. It's not like running a race, more like winning a battle of ideas.' Jenkins reached

Lord Whiffy

the top of the staircase, then turned and straddled the banister.

'Jenkins?' Joe said. 'What on earth—?'

'Whaaaaayheeeey!' Jenkins squealed as he slid at high speed back down the banister.

'I've never seen him behaving like this before,' Ajay said to Violetta as they watched from the bottom of the stairs.

'What can I say, elections are clearly Jenkins' thing,' she replied with a sigh.

'If he thinks elections are fun, he should try Chessington World of Adventures. His posh old brain would probably explode with excitement,' Ajay said.

Jenkins whooshed off the end of the banister and strode to the front door as, one by one, all the walls began to ripple and transform into computer screens. Slowly but surely, the whole house was transforming before Joe's eyes. Paintings flipped over to reveal maps complete with flashing lights, bar charts, and data screens: it was like living inside a giant Transformer.

The entire staff of No. 10 gathered around

Jenkins as he waved his hands around.

'Imagine living in a world where a duke with a trillion pounds has as much say in how the bus service should be run as, say, a man with no more than a few pennies to his name. Democracy doesn't care *who* you are, but it really is the taking part that counts. So, in answer your question, yes, we could "fill in a form", but calling a General Election should be a celebration. Democracy is coming to town!'

Joe grinned; he'd never felt so inspired. He shook Jenkins by the hand and turned round to see that everyone from the cleaner, to the chancellor, to Alice and her classmates, were all standing behind him, cheering and waving. He grinned back and then turned to the front door, knowing that he would have to do this next bit alone.

Joe stepped back out on to the doorstep of No. 10 and met a blizzard of photographers and flashing cameras once more. Taking a deep breath, he walked back to the podium to address the press for the second time that day. When Joe glanced back, Jenkins was nodding enthusiastically, and then Joe saw him pull a lever, and a robotic arm appeared carrying a cushion on which sat a ceremonial bugle. Jenkins grabbed it and puckered up before blasting out a rousing fanfare. 'BRRRRRRRRRPFFFFFFFT-TTTTTTT!'

'I have some news,' said Joe. 'We are going to have a General Election. A vote to decide if you still want me to be your Prime Minister. It turns out that due to a spot of careless admin, I am technically not your Prime Minister right now . . . I know, PLOT TWIST!' Joe paused for dramatic tension before continuing. 'If you like the way I have been running things so far, then please do vote for me, and if you would prefer Theodore Flunk as your Prime Minister, then that, of course, is your democratic right. If you vote for me, I promise I will continue to listen to you, I will do my best to fight for you, and I will make sure that we continue to be a happy and friendly nation. I promise to put our Green Space initiative at the heart of my leadership. I will make sure that every child has the chance to play, relax, and enjoy nature and plants. And I promise that we will continue to have Hats for Cats Thursdays and jelly wrestling every other Tuesday.'

Joe realized everything had gone quiet as the journalists and photographers listened to him. It gave him a surge of confidence.

'But it's all down to you,' he went on. 'You, the people, get to decide whether I keep my job or not. Whether I've been a good enough leader, or whether I've let you down. I promise that I will fight tooth and nail to earn every vote I can. I will travel up and down this great land to convince you that I can continue making this a better, fairer, happier country for one and all. I know I'm just a kid, but I have big dreams and I want to carry on making them a reality, and I'm not talking about the dream I have where I turn up late for double geography in leopard print pants.'

Joe could hardly believe he'd said all that. He saw a hundred hands shoot up in the air as the press prepared to ask questions. Joe held his hands up for calm.

'The General Election will be in two weeks' time,' he said with authority. 'Let the fun begin!'

READY, STEADY, GO!

'You heard it here first. There's going to be a General Election. That can mean only one thing. All normal programming has been cancelled. The entire TV station is now a twenty-four-seven rolling-news channel. I'm political broadcaster, Charlie James, and you're watching our ELECTION SPECIAL. We've got a big clock and we're not afraid to use it. There it is . . .' Charlie pointed behind him. 'And it's counting down each day till the election. What a fortnight it's going to be! We'll have live commentary on the race between Prime Minister Joe Perkins and old-school politician, Theodore

Flunk. We'll bring you reactions to everything that's going on, what *might* be going on, and what hasn't happened yet. And if that isn't enough, we'll also have reactions to the reactions!' Charlie threw his arm out in the direction of someone off camera. 'Hit it guys!'

Over the sound of blaring music, while garish graphics flashed on a screen behind him, Charlie James continued. 'For this Election Special, we need a special election studio, so this one has been modified so we can get up-to-the-minute updates from where the up-to-the-minute updates are happening. Yes, that's right, welcome to the world's first Heli-telly-studio, flying over the UK, from now until the election is done . . . Whoooooooa . . . bit of a wobble there . . . We're not going anywhere. And yet, WE'RE GOING EVERYWHERE! We won't be happy until every inch of this great land has been covered, until I've interviewed every man, woman, and child on the street, whether they like it or not. This is a Channel 10 news special, coming at you from the sky. There'll be a daily podcast of behind-the-scenes comment, and then another podcast about the podcast. Our promise to you is that no story will last more than three minutes. Frankly, if you can't grasp what's going on in that time frame, we're not interested. We'll have a *Strictly Come Dancing* Election Special. We'll have the *Great British Bake Off Vote Off*, where we ask both leadership candidates to bake their manifestos into cakes.'

Charlie leant over, out of breath for a moment. 'But now it's time to take to the skies . . . Don't touch that dial. This promises to be the greatest election, probably of all time!'

'Turn that racket off!' Theodore Flunk scowled in his chair in the dusty offices of the opposition party's HQ—a grey, musty building near Downing Street— where the air smelt of stale coffee and there was a constant whir of computers as teams of workers tapped away, trying to work out how to win the election.

In meeting room A, Theodore Flunk stood up and put his hands on his hips as his team of top advisors waited for him to issue instructions.

'Do you smell that?' Theodore asked them mysteriously. 'Can you whiff it?' Everyone looked at each other, confused.

'Is it my perfume?' an advisor asked, nervously chewing on her pen.

'The scotch egg I had for breakfast?' another advisor, called Johnson, asked.

'Neither,' Theodore said. 'It's victory. Victory is so close, I can smell it! It is well within our grasp! I've been waiting all my life to get to this point.' He smiled, accentuating his sharp cheekbones.

Theodore was a bony, angular man—everything about him was pointy. He had a pointy nose, pointy ears, and pointy fingers. In fact, he looked not unlike a human Toblerone.

He raised his hands to cup his ears, revealing soggy patchesonthearmpitsofhis faded mustard-coloured shirt. While his team tried to avert their eyes from the sight, Flunk continued, arrogantly. 'And can you hear that?' he asked. 'That is the sound of change.'

While everyone strained to listen to what seemed to be silence, Theodore beamed a sinister, pointy-toothed smile. 'I want this kid finished before he's even begun,' he said, before laughing menacingly, like a cartoon villain.

Power is a funny thing because it can do strange things to normal people. For some, it makes them a better person—they work harder, and become more responsible and caring. But for others, power has the opposite effect—it makes them sneaky and spiteful, and Theodore Flunk was one of those people. He didn't like to play by the rules and he wasn't in politics to make people's lives better. No, what he liked most of all was telling people what to do, making fun of people, and humiliating them. There wasn't a dodgy favour that he wouldn't call in to take down an opponent. He saw politics as a game of chess—in order for him to win, someone else had to lose. And Theodore hated losing. For too long he'd been second fiddle to Joe Perkins and it enraged him. Perkins was just a kid. How could he, Theodore Flunk, be outsmarted by a kid? Well, now was his chance! It was time for Theodore to sit at the top table. It was time for him to be Prime Minister. Annoyingly, everyone seemed to like Joe, so Theodore needed to figure out a way to turn Joe into a loser, and fast.

'We need a plan,' Theodore said to his top team, the Flunkies (that's what he called his legion of assistants.)

'Great, I'll get writing!' Johnson said.

'No, Johnson, don't write what I just said. I want us to work out the plan and *then* write it down!'

'That's why you're the boss, boss!' Johnson said.

'Right, so what's the plan? Someone tell me, so I can write it down.'

'That's what we're doing now, working out the plan. No . . . please don't write that down . . .'

Flunk sighed.

'The plan is to come up with a plan!' Johnson said re-reading his notes.

'Can someone take the pen off Johnson, he's gone silly again. Right, let's workshop some ideas, how do we get rid of Joe Perkins?'

'We could put him in a hot-air balloon and set it free?' someone suggested.

'That feels risky. Let's call it "Plan B",' Theodore said, pacing up and down.

'What if we say mean things about him?' Johnson offered, putting his hand up nervously.

'*Mean* things?' Theodore stopped pacing.

'Yeah, rather than talk about his ideas, why don't we just say mean things? You know, make him look like a right dafty?'

'Ooh, I like that. But won't that make us look like bullies?' Theodore pondered.

'Maybe, but if *someone else* said it for us, then no one would think we were the bullies. How about, you know, using journalists? You could say that if they say mean things about Joe in their newspapers, you will help them in return when you are Prime Minister?' Johnson shrugged.

'You mean, bribe some journalists to say mean things about Perkins? Promise them that once I'm in office, I'll do more sneaky favours for them?' Theodore wiggled an eyebrow.

'You're right,' Johnson shook his head. 'It's completely immoral and unethical when you say it like that.'

'No, no! It sounds brilliant,' said Theodore. 'I just wanted to make sure I had it all straight in my

head. Johnson, you may have your pen back, you have redeemed yourself!'

'Oh, thank you!' Johnson grabbed his pen back from the pot in the middle of the table. 'Can I . . .?'

'Yes, feel free to write all that down.' Theodore smiled. 'Can someone get hold of my journalist friend?' He took a swig of coffee before stifling a wet belch.

One of his assistants handed Theodore a phone. 'Des, how the dickens are you? Are you still playing squash? Is that backhand getting any better . . .? HAHAHAHAHAHA!' Theodore rolled his eyes, before cutting to the chase. 'Listen, I've got an idea. How would you like to sell a load of papers with exclusive stories from inside No. 10? You could have all that if I was Prime Minister, I just need a hand winning this election first.'

Flunk waited for the reply, drumming his fingers on the table.

'What did I have in mind? Well, a partnership. You and me working together,' he said. 'There's just one thing I need your help with first.'

THE MESSAGE

'Well that's just great,' Joe said, reading the morning's newspaper in bed. 'This article has made me look like a right doughnut.'

'What's that, Sir?' Jenkins entered the room and pushed open the curtains.

'This!' Joe said, showing Jenkins the newspaper.

PERKINS LOCKED OUT OF POWER!

Next to the headline was a picture of Joe trying to get back into Downing Street after the press conference with Alice and her classmates in tow. Jenkins read the story out loud.

Yesterday, mini Prime Minister Joe Perkins (14) was sensationally left to call an election in a desperate attempt to cling on to power. As if things couldn't get any worse for Perkins, he was locked out of No. 10— and had to ask a bunch of kids to help him open the door. At least now the public have the chance to finally vote out this imposter in favour of a real leader, like Theodore Flunk.

'Oh dear,' Perkins said, folding up the newspaper.

'OK, a few things,' Joe said. 'Firstly, I am not desperate to cling on to power. Secondly, I didn't get locked out, well, only for about a minute because, well . . . it was a misunderstanding. Thirdly, I didn't need the other kids to help me get in, and even if I did, what's wrong with that? Fourthly, I am not fourteen, though they'd probably only get more annoyed if I told them I was younger. Basically, the only thing they got right in that was my name. Can't we do anything, Jenkins? It's not fair!'

'Sadly, I fear not, Sir.'

'Well, it's not a great start to day one of the campaign.'

'Just ignore it, Sir. Concentrate on what you do best, which is connecting with people,' Jenkins said, calmly.

'You're right. So, what's the plan for today?'

'Well, you were due to go and visit an old people's home to open their new water therapy unit. You can use it as an opportunity to make a speech about the economy or something. We don't want to cancel, they've made jam tarts.'

'Ooh, yes. I like jam tarts. And I made a promise,' Joe agreed.

'Then we have a few campaign events . . . Oh, and at the end of the week, we pay a visit to Alice's neighbourhood to see the first of your new parks being built on the old bit of disused ground. It'll be a nice way to show your Green Space plan in action. We can arrange for you to plant a tree with a ceremonial spade.'

'I'm feeling better already. This is going to be a brilliant campaign, Jenksy,' Joe smiled, adding hopefully,

'Is there . . . some sort of tour bus? I've seen them on TV before, and they always look like fun. You know, a big red bus with my face on it? We can travel around spreading the word about why people should vote for me.'

'Ajay said he was organizing the transport,' Jenkins told him.

'Excuse me?'

'Yes, apparently he OK'd it with you?'

Just then, the sound of music from outside drifted through the window. Strange, high-pitched, almost shrill music. Joe narrowed his eyes, then got out of bed and walked over to the window.

'Oh dear,' said Jenkins. 'Is it what I think it is?'

'Yep, it's an ice-cream van,' Joe said, peering outside. 'And Ajay seems to be driving it.'

'Good heavens.' Jenkins stared in disbelief out of the window.

'Oi, oi LADZ!' Ajay yelled, rolling down the window. 'Say hello to the new Prime Ministerial campaign bus!'

'Stay right there!' ordered Joe, rushing to get dressed.

Standing outside, Joe and Jenkins took in the bizarre sight of a fully functioning ice-cream van that Ajay had decorated with Joe's face on the side. Clearly he'd downloaded some pictures from the internet and got them blown up at the local printers.

'My face looks distorted, Ajay,' Joe said, shaking his head. 'It's so pixelated.'

'Only up close,' Ajay said, cheerfully. 'From a distance, you can totally tell it's you. Jenkins, go and stand half a mile away and tell me what you can see.'

'No,' Jenkins said, without missing a beat.

'I look like I've been made out of Lego,' Joe shook his head. 'Also, you're not allowed to drive, Ajay, you're too young.'

'Ah, now I checked, and it's true you're not allowed to drive without a licence on a public road, but the chief of police follows me on Instagram so I asked if he could make an exception for us for the next couple of weeks and he sent me this . . .' Ajay closed one eye, like a wink, and opened the other one really wide and stuck his tongue out and stuck up a thumb. 'Which I took to mean, "yes, absolutely".'

'What *is* he doing?' Jenkins said wearily.

'He's being a human emoji,' Joe said.

'It's one of my top skills. I have memorized all of the emojis and I can re-enact them at a moment's notice.' Ajay grinned. 'Welcome aboard! We can have a whippy double-flake while I drive to the old people's home.'

Joe looked at Jenkins and shrugged. 'I sort of want to do it. I mean, I've never had my own tour bus before.'

'There's only one seat, up front with me,' Ajay said, revving the engine.

'I suppose I'll have to get in the back, then,' Jenkins sighed. 'Now promise me, Ajay. You're going to drive slowly and safely.'

'Well, I can only really drive one way, as anyone who's ever seen me play *Forza Horizon 7* will testify.'

'Play what?' Jenkins said, squeezing into the back of the van to sit amongst the ice-cream and sauces.

'It's a racing game! Hold on, Jenksy!' Joe yelled,

as Ajay floored the van and sped off.

'WHAAAAAA!' Jenkins screamed as a box of flakes hit him squarely in the face. He tried to pull himself up from the floor and grabbed what he thought was the door handle, but it turned out to be the nozzle for the ice-cream, which splattered everywhere, before a box of hundreds-and-thousands landed on his ice-cream-soaked head.

'Nice one, Jenkins! I'll have a nobbly bobbly,' Ajay said. 'Shall we put some music on?'

'How? I can't see a stereo,' Joe said, as he was forced back into his seat.

'Stereo?' Ajay said, hitting a button. Suddenly, the shrill sounds of the ice-cream van siren blasted out "We Are The Champions" at full volume, as the van swerved out of Downing Street and headed in the direction of the old people's home. 'This is the only way to travel, eh my man?'

'Well, it certainly makes a change,' Joe beamed.

'Is that a box of Magnums sellotaped to your foot?'

'It's the only way I can reach the brakes.'

'So you are aware that this thing has brakes?' Jenkins shouted, as a pot of fluorescent strawberry sauce landed on his head.

'Lol!' Ajay replied. 'Now settle down, we'll be there in twenty minutes or so.'

One and a half hours later, after Jenkins had explained the difference between clockwise and anti-clockwise to Ajay, everyone emerged from the campaign bus a little green around the gills and with a lot of ice-cream splattered about their person.

'Look at me, I'm a mess, there's hundreds-and-thousands everywhere,' Joe said, dusting himself down.

'Relax. I've organized a change of costume for you . . .' said Ajay, breezily.

'Costume?' Joe asked.

'Yeah. Politicians always talk down to old people, but you're young and fresh. You can make all this stuff about the economy really interesting. Liven it up a bit, you know, for all the journalists.' Ajay pointed at a bunch of reporters and photographers waiting outside the home. 'So, in the middle of the night I had a brilliant idea.' Ajay handed a bag of clothes to Joe and a box of records to Jenkins.

'What on earth—?' Joe peered into the bag and pulled out a baseball cap.

'How do you feel about rapping?' Ajay said, grinning.

'YO, YO, YO!' Ajay boomed into the microphone. 'I JUST WANNA SAY BIG UP TO ALL MY HOMIES OUT THERE. I AM M.C. AJAY, DA BIGGEST, DA BESTEST, DA BADDEST HYPE MAN ON DA SCENE. AND I AM HERE TO INTRODUCE J. MASTER P. YOU MAY KNOW HIM AS DA PRIME MINISTER, BUT TAKE AWAY THE SUIT AND THE BRIEFCASE AND YOU GOT DA BADDEST FLY BOY FROM DA MEAN STREETS. MY MAN IS HERE TO TALK

INTEREST RATE LEVELS. TAKE IT AWAY D.J. JENKINS, SPIN DA WHEELS OF STEEL. DROP SOME DOPE AND SIC BEATS!'

Joe, standing in the large living room of the old people's home, stared in horror at his friend, as Ajay turned to Jenkins and lowered his voice.

'Press the button on the turntable, Jenksy. Like we rehearsed.'

Jenkins was kitted out in a baseball cap and a black silk tracksuit, with gold chains dangling round his neck, looking supremely uncomfortable. He nodded and hit the button on the keyboard as instructed. The air was instantly filled with thundering drum and bass beats. There were a dozen flashes as the press at the back of the room took pictures and started filming.

'AYE, AYE!' Joe began to freestyle, looking terrified. 'I JUST WANNA SAY, THANK YOU FOR INVITING ME AND ME MAD CREW TO DA OPENING OF DA NEW WATER THERAPY UNIT AT DA MEADOW HILL NURSING HOME. DIS IS HOW I ROLL . . . DROP DA BASE, AND

WHEN I SAY BASE, I MEAN BASE LEVEL OF THE INTEREST RATES. COZ THEY IS OF NO INTEREST TO ME, MATE. DA WAY I SEE IT, WE NEED TO INCREASE EXPORTATION OF MY MANUFACTURING CONNECTION TO KEEP INFLATION FROM SWAYIN' OUT OF CONTROL, MY CONGREGATION . . .' Settling into the rap a bit, Joe started flouncing around, waving his hands to the largely confused group of pensioners, while cameras snapped and reporters scribbled furiously in their notepads.

'Put some effort into it!' Ajay mouthed. 'Do something unexpected.'

Joe nodded, flinging his arms about like a real rapper, throwing the mic from one hand to the other and missing by a mile. Then he and Ajay watched, open-mouthed, as the microphone flew through the air and, with a big, booming thud, struck an old lady called Pearl right on the noggin.

THINGS CAN ONLY GET BETTER

JOE PERKINS WALLOPS A PENSIONER!

Joe sighed, reading the newspaper the next day.

Joe Perkins promised to connect with the electorate yesterday, but little did they know, that meant having a microphone thrown at them. Pearl (82) said 'I'm 82 you know!' Joe (12) has had a disastrous start to the campaign, following a very slick event by Theodore Flunk.

Joe sighed again, putting the paper down.

'They've got my age wrong again. And I didn't *throw* a microphone. It sort of just flew out of my hand. Why couldn't they report the bit where I took Pearl to lunch to say sorry, and how afterwards she and I got involved in a freestyle rap battle, which I know she enjoyed. This journalist has it in for me. When I do something nice, they call me soft or weak. When I try and be tough about something, they call me "bossy". Whatever I do, they twist and turn it. I mean, look at that picture they used, of me looking ridiculous eating that sausage roll. Admittedly, the

JOE PERKINS
WALLOPS A
PENSIONER

rap costume's not helping, but that's beside the point!' Joe slammed the paper down and looked around the room at his team of ministers. There was Jim from Health and Social Care, Angela the Chancellor, and Violetta Crump, Joe's deputy.

'Would you like one of my kiwi fruits?' Violetta asked. 'They always make me feel better whenever I'm feeling tetchy or down.'

'No, thank you,' Joe sighed. 'I just can't seem to catch a break. The papers have definitely got it in for me.'

'I can't help feeling this is partly my fault,' Ajay chipped in. 'You know, the rapping and all that.'

'You think?' Joe rolled his eyes, but then smiled at his friend. 'No, it's not your fault. I agreed to go along with it and I think everyone actually had fun in the end. It feels as though it doesn't matter what I do, they'll always be digging up the negative stuff. We can't win.'

Just then, there was a knock at the door. 'Come in,' Joe said miserably.

'Sorry, Sir. I couldn't stop her—I said you were

in a meeting . . .' Joe's secretary said, coming into the room, closely followed by Joe's mum.

'Where is he? Where's my little soldier? Come on, give your mum a big hug!'

'Oh, hi, Mum,' Joe said, blushing and trying to escape her clutches as she came in for a hug. 'I'm sort of in the middle of something here—'

'Now, don't you pay any attention to that mean journalist. You're not a wiry-haired loser. They don't know Mummy's little prince, not like I do.'

As some of the team tittered, Ajay grabbed the newspaper and leafed through it.

'Page 5, paragraph 6, dear,' Joe's mum clarified.

'Thanks, Mum,' Joe said, wondering which was more humiliating—being called a wiry-haired loser—or Mummy's little prince.

'Now, I've made your favourite dinner. Vegetarian chili con carne, and custard for dessert.'

Mrs Perkins plonked a Tupperware box down on the table.

'Mum. It's nine in the morning,' Joe said. 'It's a bit early for . . .'

He stopped and stared intently at the box of food.

'I only had one box, so I bunged the custard in with the chilli,' she explained.

While Joe looked queasy, Ajay grabbed the Tupperware and a fork and began tucking in to the spicy chilli and custard.

'Right. So what exactly are we going to do about those knuckleheads at the paper? I won't have them talking about my boy like that.' She pulled something out of her bag. 'This'll do for a start, I did it on the bus over here.'

They were looking at a placard which had JOE PERKINS IS MY LITTLE SHNOOKUMS. LEAVE HIM BE!! scrawled on it in red paint.

'Oh my Gawd.' Joe slumped down into his seat. 'This is not a good idea, Mum. The Prime Minister can't send his mother to fight his battles. It doesn't look good!'

'We need to fight fire with fire,' Mrs Perkins yelled.

'Actually, your mum is right,' Violetta said, standing up.

Joe's mum's eyes narrowed. 'I know you, Violetta Crump. And I don't trust you,' she hissed.

'That's as maybe, but we need to work together if Joe is going to win this election.' Violetta's voice was strident. 'I think we can all agree on that, can't we?'

'I suppose so.' Mrs Perkins sighed and Ajay nodded.

'In order to win,' said Violetta, 'we need to fight dirty.'

'Fight dirty!' Ajay said, nearly choking on his custard. 'But that's not what we do!'

Joe looked down at the paper and sighed another big sigh. 'Let's just hear her out.'

'Thank you Prime Minister,' said Violetta. 'The thing is, you're too nice. It's often a great strength, but sometimes you need to play another game. Like the game Theodore and his little journalist friend are playing. They are going to win this election by playing dirty.' She put her hands on her hips and stared at

Joe. 'Do you really want to be forever branded as that "annoying, spotty little brat, who with his greedy side-kick is running this country into the ground"?'

'Wha—?' Joe asked.

'Page 7, paragraph 12.' Violetta held out the newspaper.

'I don't need to read it. I take your point,' said Joe. 'But how do you know Theodore is even involved?'

'Oh, don't be so naïve Joe! Everyone in politics knows the two are in cahoots.'

'Sir, I don't think this is the right way to go,' said Jenkins.

'I'm not agreeing to anything, Jenksy. I just want to hear Violetta's plan.'

'Well . . .' Violetta said carefully. 'It's not even "playing dirty" as such, but instead, simply playing them at their own game a bit, so that you can get your point across without all these awful stories about you clouding people's judgement. I happen to know someone who can help. Does the name "The Rottweiler" ring any bells?'

WHO LET THE DOGS OUT?

'Explain to me again why we're in an ice-cream van, speeding through the countryside to meet a man named after a dog, all before nine thirty in the morning?' Joe asked.

'He's the best there is and he has never lost an election,' Violetta said, squeezed in the back of the van next to Ajay and Joe. Luckily, Jenkins was driving, having confiscated the keys from Ajay.

'I watched a documentary about The Rottweiler once. He's also known as the "election whisperer". No one really knows what he looks like, he stays in the background, but he's really cool, sort of like Batman, except he's named after a dog!' Ajay grinned.

'Wow,' Joe said.

'I know,' Ajay said.

'No, I mean, "wow", that you were watching a documentary.'

'I'm more than just a pretty face, you know,' said Ajay.

'He does have a fearsome reputation, I will admit,' Jenkins said, turning a little to join in. He took one hand off the steering wheel and carefully passed Joe a file marked "Classified Information". 'I took the liberty of doing a bit of checking before we set off, though I couldn't find much information about him. He was born in Australia and has a rugged, no-nonsense style about him, though he protects his anonymity well. In the file, you'll see one of the few pictures of him I could find. And his real name is Jim Jones.'

'Why does he look so angry?' Joe asked, studying the picture of a grumpy-faced middle-aged man.

'Because he's a winner?' Ajay said.

'And winning makes him angry?' Joe asked.

'No, being angry makes him a winner. I suppose he's only happy when he's angry.' Ajay smiled, pleased with this insight.

'That makes no sense at all,' Joe said. 'Anyway. How do you know him, Violetta?'

'Oh, he's helped me out with a few election campaigns in the past.'

'I have to say, Sir,' Jenkins interjected, 'I have grave concerns about this man. Yes, he's a winner, but at what cost?'

'Look, it's just a meeting,' said Joe. 'Yes, I'm concerned a bit by this guy's reputation, but at the same time, I know in my heart of hearts that Theodore Flunk would be a terrible Prime Minister. And I know I'm not perfect but have you seen what he said he would do if he wins the election? He wants to serve broccoli with every school meal, introduce triple maths lessons and ban break times. Flunk obviously really hates kids—imagine making everyone eat broccoli!'

'Your feelings on the green vegetable are well known, Sir. I just think we need to exercise a bit of caution,' Jenkins said, pulling into the long drive of Jim Jones's house.

'Obviously,' Joe said. 'But he has a 100% success rate and I just want to know what his secret is.'

'Well, whatever his secret is,' Jenkins said, 'it's certainly made him very rich.'

Joe looked out of the window at the grand house ahead. It looked like something from a horror movie. Tall, gothic, dark, and imposing. There were creepy gargoyles staring at him from every angle. It was the kind of place that might be haunted.

As the van came to a stop and they all got out, the air felt colder, the clouds felt thicker and heavier. Everyone gulped.

'Please tell me he's expecting us?' Joe asked, staring at a sign that read *Trespassers Will Be Electrocuted*.

'Oh, yes. Jim's a teddy bear really. This is all for show,' Violetta said as the four of them approached the front door.

'It's open,' Joe said, pushing the large wooden door. It made a creaking sound like a wounded animal. 'Well that's not creepy, at all.'

'I think I may wet my pants,' Ajay trembled.

'Imagine having this much money and wanting to live in a gloomy place like this,' Joe said, as they walked through into the marble hall.

'Nothing in this world makes sense!' A low voice rumbled from the shadows.

'Mr . . . Rottweiler?' Joe called out.

'Yeah . . .' A figure came forward from the shadows like a vampire emerging from its sleep.

'Please don't hurt us, I squeal like a toddler and can scratch like a cat!' Ajay yelled, pulling a taekwondo training move.

'Eh?' The voice said, switching on the lights. 'Listen, mate, I'm not going to hurt you.'

A gruff man in a disheveled suit stepped into the hall. He had receding hair and a face which was bright pink, as though his skin was prickling with anger. He also had wide, staring eyes and a thick field of stubble on his face, along with a big, bushy moustache. 'Why don't you come in?' he smiled as he showed them the way to the living room and nodded at Violetta, who nodded back.

'It's good to see you Jim, it's been a while.' Violetta grinned.

'It's been too long, V,' Jim said. 'You haven't changed a bit. Are you still eating your political enemies for breakfast?'

'Oh no, I have utterly and completely changed. I'm now into smoothies and yoga.' Violetta smiled.

'Er, this is quite a . . .' Joe trailed off as he looked around the room they were in.

'OH MY WORD!' Ajay squealed. 'LOOK AT ALL THIS TECHNOLOGY. CAN WE WORK WITH THE ROTTWEILER, PLEASE JOE, PLEASE?'

Ajay walked wide-eyed past supercomputer after supercomputer. It was like the high-tech lair of a super villain.

'I'm glad you like it. I find it very restful,' Jim smiled. 'Drinks?' He nodded at one of his many assistants who were creeping around the joint like human spiders, all dressed in black.

'Yes, thank you. I'd like a coffee,' Jenkins said. 'Milk, no sugar, please.'

'Sure,' Jim said. 'Come through to the brainstorm hub. It's where we can all plug into the ideas factory and shoot the breeze.'

Joe, Jenkins, Ajay, and Violetta walked through a strange combination of the old and new, as computers and high tech met with gothic and grand. More people wearing nothing but black tapped away on keyboards, looking secretive and important.

It felt like lifting the bonnet off the internet and having a look around inside.

'Wow, look at all this stuff,' Ajay said. 'Can you play *Fortnite* on one of those things?'

'Nah. What we do is way more fun than that,' Jim smiled. 'We shape people's lives and change the destiny of the world by using all of humankind as though they are one giant computer game,' Jim said, proudly.

'WOW. OK, IT IS COOLER!' Ajay gushed.

'Thanks for seeing us at such short notice,' Joe said, trying hard not to seem too impressed.

'No problem, kid. Just don't start rapping at me,' Jim replied, leading them through a glass door, into a futuristic-style meeting room.

'Oh, you saw that?' Joe said, blushing.

'Hard to miss it. Kind of thing the newspapers have a field day with. And not just them.' Jim picked up an iPad. 'You've been trending on social media all day.'

'That's a good thing, right?' Joe smiled, and then he looked more closely at the screen.

'"Hashtag Joe's cRAP,"' he read. 'That's harsh. Then again, look at all those hits.'

'I know. Amazing, right?' Jim patted him on the shoulder and winked. 'Joe, instead of waiting for the news media to give the people a story, you have to get in there first and spin the story yourself. I call it THE 360 DEGREE MATRIX NEWSOLUTION!' Jim pressed a button on a remote control and a hologram popped up from the middle of the table. 'We get most of our news from the internet these days and that's where I come in.' He gestured around him. 'Using all this clever technology, I help people to make up their minds about things!'

'But that's not reporting the news, that's manipulation!' Jenkins snapped, turning to Joe. 'Sir, I think we should go. What happened to good old-fashioned talking to people and explaining your ideas to them face to face?'

'This *is* talking to people,' said Jim, patiently. 'With technology, we can talk to an entire country at once. We can run opinion polls to find out what people think of Joe, and what they want from a leader, and then we can feed them all the right messages to win their vote. It's a kind of science.'

'But how?' Ajay asked, his eyes wide with wonder.

'Well, who here has a phone?' Jim asked, and everyone put their hand up.

At this point, one of his assistants walked in with a coffee for Jenkins and some Ribena for Joe and Ajay.

'Our favourite drink . . .' Ajay said, taking a sip. 'But how did you know?'

'Get your phones out and I'll show you.'

One by one, small black rectangles were slapped down on the table.

'One, two . . . right, who's not put their phone down?' Jim asked. There was a loud thud as Jenkins put his on the table.

'Wow!' Ajay said, 'that's huge.'

'It's from 1999,' said Jenkins defensively. 'People mock but I paid good money for that phone, and it's still going strong. The battery alone can go for nearly seven months without needing a recharge.'

They all stared down at the shoebox-sized phone.

'It's bigger than my laptop,' Ajay said, shaking his head.

'All right, let's see yours,' Jim asked.

Ajay opened his jacket and popped another phone down, then rolled up his trouser leg and pulled out a third phone from his ankle holster. 'Nearly there,' Ajay said, checking his other jacket pocket and producing another device. 'And, one more . . .' He lifted up his baseball cap.

'You have *five* phones?' Jenkins said.

'I'm very important. Anyway, all of my phones put together are still smaller than yours.'

'Everything we do is on our phone. It knows where we've been, what games we like, clothes, food, drink, who our friends are, and what we've been looking at online.' Jim paused. 'Well, obviously not yours, Jenkins mate, yours is safe, but everyone else's has tons of information about them on it.'

'Really?' Joe asked.

'Wait, how?' Ajay asked.

Jim picked up one of Ajay's smartphones and opened it. 'Look, here on Instagram—"time for squash!" And a boring photo of your baseball cap. A few hashtags, too, #timeforribena, #biscuittime, #parched, #iliketodunkitdunkitiliketodunkitdunkit; there's also your location. Now your phone knows what you like to drink, what type of biscuit you like, and in fact, yep, here are a load of adverts for biscuits in your timeline. I know everything about you just from looking at your social media feed, what ice-cream you like, your favourite pop star. How Jenkins is allergic to cats . . .'

'What?' Jenkins asked.

'I took a secret Boomerang when you had that sneezing fit, it was totally hilarious,' Ajay laughed.

'We can use all this data to help us win votes. We know what the voters want before they do. We can test and retest ideas twenty-four hours a day, creating a hub of voters in real time,' Jim said.

'Impressive,' Violetta smiled.

'But what about meeting real people, and listening to what they want?' Jenkins asked. 'That's what Joe does best.'

'He'll still meeting real people, but they'll be real

people who are already on board with his message,' Jim shrugged.

Joe looked unsure.

'It's the new reality, mate. If you want to win you have to play this game,' said Jim. 'We want the good guy, that's you, to win, right? If you employ me, we can check in with the public to make sure your ideas are getting across nice and clearly. Not a speech will be delivered without us checking every word. You don't put a pair of socks on before telling me. Every thought, idea, and every decision will be run by me. And then I promise you will win this election and can concentrate on listening to the public after that. But it's up to you, Joe. Do you want to run your campaign your way and let Theodore Flunk win, or do you want to do it my way, and win?'

While Joe looked a bit overwhelmed by Jim's speech, Violetta got to her feet.

'I have to use the little girl's room,' she said. 'And you have a decision to make, Joe.'

Joe looked around the room. Ajay was smiling and nodding, still overawed by the tech; Jenkins looked far less convinced, but then Jenkins was old-school. He was brilliant, Joe thought, but a little stuck in the past, whereas Jim had a solid plan to beat Theodore, even if Joe didn't properly understand it. Maybe this was just how elections worked?

Suddenly, Jim's phone rang. He reached out and grabbed it, studying the number flashing up on the screen.

'Theodore Flunk,' he said. 'Someone must have given him my number. Obviously I can't work for *both* political candidates . . .' Jim shot a sly look at Joe. 'So you'd better make your mind up, kid. Should I answer this call, or am I working for you?'

Joe gulped. What choice did he have if he wanted to keep doing the job he loved more than anything else in the world?

'No. Don't answer the phone,' Joe said hastily. 'Welcome to my election campaign.'

'I'll pick you up first thing in the morning,' Jim winked at Joe. 'Pack a bag, kid. Tomorrow this election campaign really begins.'

ICE, ICE BABY

'Oopsy!' Violetta said as they left Jim's place. 'I forgot my handbag, back in a minute.'

'OK, well, let's have an ice-cream while we wait, I think we've earned it,' Joe said to Jenkins and Ajay. 'Plus I need to FaceTime Alice and give her an update.'

Alice came into view on Joe's phone.

'Hi Alice! Look, Ajay and Jenksy are here too.'

'Hey Alice!' Ajay said, holding a Cornetto on top of his head. 'Look, I'm a unicorn!'

'We're still really looking forward to launching the Green Space initiative in a few days. We just employed the best in the business to work on my election campaign so I'm feeling really good about my chances on election day. And in the meantime, we could turn up to your road with diggers and make that piece of land near your house into a park, to show people just what we can achieve. We can plant some trees, too. How does that sound?' Joe sat back.

'Perfect, thanks, Prime Minister,' Alice said, smiling. 'The sooner the better. People are using it to dump rubbish. Look!' She turned her phone round to show a pile of old mattresses and a shopping trolley. 'Isn't it awful?'

'My goodness,' Jenkins said. 'Why would people do that?'

'I don't know,' Joe sighed. 'Well, it won't be like that for long. We'll get the press along and make it into a real celebration of green spaces.'

'Say no more, boss. I'm on it!' Ajay said, tapping his nose.

'Well, actually, I wasn't really asking for your help, Ajay,' Joe said.

'You don't even need to ask twice, bro, it goes

'without saying,' Ajay grinned.

'Well, I'm super excited for it all to get going,' said Alice. 'We're miles from any other park. I thought maybe we could grow flowers and vegetables there too, and make a community garden?'

'Oh, I like that idea,' Joe smiled. 'Pass me a Cornetto, Ajay. Go on, Alice . . .'

'You forget something, V?' Jim said, as Violetta entered the room.

'Just this.' She grabbed her bag. 'Oh, and to say thank you, I really think with your help victory will be ours . . . oops, sorry. Did I say "ours"? I meant mine.'

Jim laughed. 'I tell you what, that phone call from "Flunk" was genius!'

'Well, the child needed a little push. I mean, I knew we had Ajay on board. He's like a magpie, show him anything big and shiny and you've got him, every time,' Violetta said, pacing Jim's office.

'I'm curious, though,' Jim said. 'I'm used to

thinking three steps ahead of my opponents, but you were about fifteen steps ahead. How did you come up with the plan?'

'How did I come up with the plan? Well, I've had a lot of time to think recently. My word, I've been so bored. Drinking all those smoothies, and doing all that hugging.' She shuddered. 'It's disgusting being that nice. Never, ever try it. Percival T. Duckholm always was a fool and I just knew he must have made some sort of mistake when he handed over power to the kid, so I went and checked. Bingo!' She laughed with delight. 'I leaked the error to the press, knowing that Joe would be forced to call a General Election or resign. Theodore Flunk has been playing his part of course, though he doesn't know that I am the one making all of this happen. And then, all I had to do was steer Joe towards hiring you for the campaign. I really think we've got him this time!'

'Oh, you're a ruthless woman, Violetta Crump,' said Jim. 'I like it. Before long we'll have that kid doing and saying everything we tell him to.'

'With your help, Joe will ruin his image and his political career. And that's when I will save the day. I will step in and nobly step up to lead the party myself. It's too perfect!'

'Aren't you worried about Theodore Flunk? What if you lose to him?'

'We'll deal with him when the time is right,' Violetta said, confidently.

'And Jenkins?' said Jim. 'He's on to me already, V. He may be the biggest threat to our plan.'

'Yes, that worries me, too. But the very fact that Jenkins is such a stubborn old dinosaur may well work in our favour . . .' Violetta grabbed a cigar from a box on Jim's desk. 'Do you mind? I'll save this to celebrate my first day in office at No. 10 Downing Street.'

'Take it,' said Jim. 'It'll remind you what you promised to do for me, Violetta. Make me Head of Communications, with a big, fat salary to match.

Imagine, you get to control an entire country. Imagine what we could make them do!'

'Jim, my dear, old friend. If we pull this off, your every wish is my command. I just want that do-gooding kid gone. No more driving around in an ice-cream van, smiling and talking to people. No more being kind, and please, no more laughing. Laughter makes me want to pull my own teeth out,' Violetta grimaced.

'That's the spirit.' Jim nodded in approval and tilted his coffee cup at her in a toast. 'Here's to all-out victory in a week's time, and defeating the child Prime Minister, once and for all!'

MAGICAL MYSTERY TOUR

'What time did he say he'd be here?' Jenkins asked.

'He didn't,' Joe said, feeling a little bit apprehensive. On the other hand, it did feel nice not to be in charge for once. Having someone else make all the decisions was reassuring. It felt like the beginning of a new adventure. Jim Jones was going to save his campaign and then Joe could get back to the job he loved most in the world.

'Yoo-hoo! I didn't know what to pack, so I thought I'd travel light,' Ajay said, dragging a huge suitcase towards Joe and Jenkins.

'You call that light?' Jenkins asked.

'Most of this is toiletries to be honest,' Ajay beamed. 'It takes an awful lot of effort to look this good!'

Joe turned to Violetta, who stood with a tiny wheelie suitcase next to her. 'I'm so glad you're on board with us,' he told her. 'We could do with your experience, not to mention your valuable contacts. Now that you've introduced us to The Rottweiler, we're on our way!'

'My pleasure, Prime Minister.' She smiled. 'I've packed some herbal juice for us all. It's my own recipe.'

'It looks like a pint of sneeze,' Ajay said, shaking his head. 'I'll pass, thanks.'

'Each to their own,' Violetta smiled. 'Ah, our ride's here.'

The sight that greeted them took Joe's breath away. It was the most incredible bus he'd ever seen. It was like a coach and a spaceship had been welded together and stretched to the size of an aircraft carrier. It was gigantic!

There was a screech as the vehicle came to a thundering stop, and a loud hiss as the air breaks kicked in. Then there was another hiss and a puff of steam as the door seemed to float open and a set of stairs descended to the ground. It was just like a UFO had landed on earth.

'Say hello to your new battlebus.' Suddenly, Jim appeared through a mist of steam and Joe took a step back to see what was plastered all over the side of the bus. It was his face, giant and clear, with the slogan 'Winning for Britain' underneath in sleek, professional lettering.

'Cool!' cried Ajay. 'This is almost as good as the ice-cream van!'

'Wow. I mean, wow,' said Joe, trying to take it all in. The coach was so big that it could barely fit on the road outside No. 10. 'You really don't hang about, Jim. How did you knock up a bus like this in twenty-four hours? What a way to get around the country!'

'And who exactly is paying for this monstrosity?' Jenkins said, wrinkling his nose.

'Don't you worry about that, Jenkins, It's all

part of the service. And opinion polls show that people are more likely to vote for someone who has a big bus,' Jim cackled. 'But don't think of this as merely a bus. This is a nerve centre on wheels! It's a political control unit, a giant, mobile laptop capable of pumping out our message twenty-four hours a day, seven days a week. It's a living, breathing information beast, it's a home, it's a hotel, it's a TV studio, it's a think tank, it's—'

'It's got a toilet and everything!' Ajay said, bursting back out of the door, 'I mean a real proper bog. Not just fit for number ones, but number twos, too, you could probably do a number five and six in there and it could take it!'

'What's a number five and six?' Jim Jones asked.

'You really don't want to know,' said Joe. 'And if I told you, you'd wish I hadn't.'

'It's a bit ostentatious,' Jenkins said. 'I mean, is it really *us*?'

'Us?' Joe asked, walking up to the door of the bus.

'Yes, you're the ordinary boy-next-door Prime Minister. You listen to people on the streets, like

Alice, and you take action,' Jenkins said, following Joe inside.

'It's still us, but just with a state-of-the-art campaign bus,' said Joe. 'Like new and improved cola!'

'All I'm doing, Jenkins, is making sure that Joe has everything he needs to win this election. Come and look inside,' Jim said. 'These are your workers, spreading our message and running polls to find out what people really want, so we can give it to them.'

'Yes, you do keep saying that,' Jenkins muttered.

The interior of the bus was as luxurious as the outside. There were plush, cream leather seats and a bar to serve hot drinks and snacks. They walked up a winding staircase, arriving on the top deck, which was filled with more of Jim's assistants, all glued to computer screens, processing and inputing data. Joe smiled at them all and waved.

'Thanks for coming on board, I really appreciate all this help,' he said, but they barely looked up to acknowledge him.

'Don't take it personally. They're wired into the information matrix, you can't stop them, or interrupt them,' Jim said.

Joe, Ajay, Violetta, and Jenkins moved downstairs again. At the back of the bus were four bedrooms and two bathrooms, a games room to relax in, and even a TV studio to do live interviews from. This bus had everything they needed. It was like taking a town on tour.

'What's through there?' Joe asked, looking at a door further back.

'Oh, you're going to love this,' said Jim. 'This is where you become the new you.'

'What?' Joe asked.

'Go on in and introduce yourself,' Jim said.

Joe walked nervously towards the door. He turned round and looked at Ajay, who shrugged his shoulders, as if to say, 'Don't ask me'. Joe took a deep breath and slowly turned the handle. He paused to peer inside but he couldn't make out a thing. The room was pitch-black.

'Hello . . .' Joe said, cautiously. Suddenly, he felt something pounce on him. 'WHAAAAA!' he screamed. 'HEEEEELP!' Something flung him upside down. Then two hands grabbed an arm each, and another two seized hold of his legs. He was apparently being attacked by a person with four arms—or was it two people? It didn't really matter, it was horrible either way. Joe felt his life flash in front of his eyes. Was this the end? Was the fat lady singing? Was it goodnight world, nice knowing you? He was frozen in fear, caught in the grip of the unknown.

But before he knew it, all the lights came on. He looked down to see that it wasn't a four-armed maniac, not even two maniacs. Nope, Joe was being man-handled by a load of robot hands. They had flung him around like a chef spinning a piece of pizza dough.

'WELCOME TO MAKE-OVER 3000, THE FUTURE OF IMAGE UPGRADES. YOU ARE ABOUT TO BECOME A BETTER YOU!' a robotic voice bleated.

Joe looked over to see an observation window, behind which Ajay, Violetta, Jenkins, and Jim were stood, staring in at him and grinning.

'Why are you smiling? This isn't funny!' Joe said as he was spun around and around. With the lights on, the room resembled a small car wash, with a production line of robotic hands all coming at him. 'NOOO!' Joe yelled, as a thing with hands like scissors came hurtling towards him.

'INITIATING HAIRCUT SEQUENCE,' it boomed.

'Chill out, Joe,' Jim said, speaking through the intercom. 'You're about to get the mother of all make-overs. When you come out, you'll look like a whole new version of yourself. For instance, we've run stats on many styles of haircut through our big computer and we have found out the exact hairstyle which people find most trustworthy.'

'Relax?' Joe yelled, just as he felt something move beneath him. He looked down to see he was on a conveyor belt. 'Where am I going?!'

As he slowly moved with the belt, a whole new batch of arms dropped down from the ceiling, one brandishing a nail file, one with moisturizer, and powder to do his make-up, and another that was thrusting a toothbrush into his mouth. Now Joe could only grunt as a robot shuffled forward and removed his shirt and trousers, replacing them with a smart pinstriped suit.

'We worked out what shoes you need to wear and how to tie your shoelaces, which shade of dark blue your suit should be—we even had a team working all night on the size of the pinstripes. The make-up is to hide any spots and blemishes, and we've got you the world's most irresistible deodorant—environmentally sound, of course. You'll look and smell as fresh as a daisy by the time we're done,' Jim smiled.

The others watched through the window as robots pushed, pulled, plucked, suited, booted, polished, and buffed Joe in every way possible. By the time they were done, Joe was dumped in front of a full-length mirror, and was barely able to recognize himself.

Dazed, confused, and minty fresh, Joe opened the door and stumbled out.

'Perfect!' Jim smiled. 'Just perfect. I created the whole procedure myself. Now, you are the optimum version of Joe Perkins. From your skin, to your hair, to your smile, and finally your clothes.'

'Can you do me next?' Ajay giggled. 'Can you make me look like Thor?'

'I'm afraid not, this is for Joe only.'

'Oh, man, that sucks.' Ajay made his smile turn dramatically upside down and did a weird blinking thing with his eyes.

Jim frowned at him. 'Is . . . he OK?'

'Oh, Ajay's being a human emoji again. Get used to it.' Joe rolled his eyes. 'Anyway, what happens next?'

'Well, we have the Green Space initiative you're so keen on in a couple of days, and a few campaign events before that. But first, we visit Kettering.' Jim smiled.

'Kettering?' Joe asked. 'Why?'

'A lion!' Jim smiled enigmatically.

THE LION (DOESN'T) SLEEP TONIGHT

The campaign bus pulled up outside Kettering Zoo and the eagerly awaiting press pack. Joe stood nervously in the doorway, looking left and right for any dangerous wild animals as he tiptoed down the steps to the ground.

'The lion isn't outside in the car park, Joe,' said Jim, who was right behind him.

'Well, you can't be too sure. Some lions can be very wily. I've seen them on TV, on those nature shows, concealing themselves amongst—'

'What? Ford Mondeos?' Jim said quietly. 'The

point is that lions are scary. You standing next to one, or feeding a steak to one, makes you look brave and decisive. You're not scared, Joe Perkins. You were born to rule! You're the man! It's a perfect way to kick-off this new-look campaign.'

'Yes, but I'm not a man, I'm a boy,' Joe pointed out. 'And frankly, I don't think there's anything wrong with being afraid of lions. It's not like being afraid of door knobs, or the colour blue. Lions are *supposed* to be scary, because if you get close to them they'll probably tear you to shreds. Being afraid of lions is actually very sensible.'

'Oh come on, Joe. It's just like a normal trip to the zoo, except this time you get to climb in a cage with the animals,' Ajay said, jumping off the bus. 'And as your image adviser, I must advise you that it will be good for your image.'

Jim patted Ajay on the shoulder. 'Thanks, but *I'm* Joe's image consultant now. I've got it from here.'

'Right, Joe. In that case, I'm advising you to follow Jim's image advice.' Ajay tapped his nose and winked at Jim.

'Ajay,' called Violetta sweetly. 'I could murder another coffee. Maybe you could organize some lattes for everyone?'

'On it!' Ajay beamed.

Joe waved and smiled at the crowd of people gathered outside the zoo. 'Hello! Thanks for coming!'

'No problem. Well worth it for a tenner,' said one man, patting his pocket.

'What's he talking about?' Joe whispered to Jim.

'Oh, nothing for you to worry about,' Jim whispered back. 'Come and meet the zookeeper!'

'Lovely to meet you!' Joe said, shaking the zoo-keeper's hand. 'I'm Joe.'

'Gareth,' the zookeeper smiled back.

'Wow, so fierce,' Joe said, looking through the bars at the lions.

'Look, what you've got to remember is that lions get a bad press. Really, they're mostly harmless,' said Gareth.

'Um, OK.' Joe swallowed. 'Listen, Gareth. I can't

help noticing that you've only got one leg. Nothing to do with the lions I hope!'

'Lattes for everyone!' Ajay interrupted, behind them. Joe briefly turned to see his friend handing out the hot drinks to Jenkins, Jim, and Violetta, before he turned back to Gareth.

'Well?'

Gareth shrugged. 'Occupational hazard, and it wasn't *this* lion. Not Blossom. It was Blossom's old mum, Mummy Blossom.'

'Blossom?' Joe asked, nervously.

'Blossom.' The zookeeper pointed behind him to the wheezing, drooling lion that had crept up to the bars.

'JOE.WHHHHHHACHOOOOOOOOOOOO!' Jenkins bellowed, sneezing and spitting out his coffee all over Violetta. 'Oops, I'm so sorry!' he mouthed as everyone turned round to stare at him.

'Let me mop that down for you, Violetta,' Ajay said, grabbing a hanky from his pocket.

'GET OFF ME, I'M FINE!' Violetta shrieked, before remembering her calming breathing exercises.

'So, how long have you been zookeeping, Gareth?' Joe asked, nervously.

'A year or two really, I sort of fell into the trade,' Gareth shrugged.

'Fell into zookeeping? How? What did you do before?'

'I was a plumber.'

'What?' Joe said, panicking. 'Surely it takes years of training to look after wild animals?'

'Nah. They give you a pamphlet and then it's a half-day session on the basics,' Gareth said. 'Yeah, funny story, really. I only came to fix the radiators in the zoo's ticket office, and that's when I saw the vacancy on the notice board: "ZOO KEEPER WANTED". That's when my life changed forever.' He grinned, as Joe glanced anxiously down at where his leg should have been.

'Shall we go in?' Gareth grabbed a steak from a tray and handed it to Joe.

'OK, I'm about to go in!' Joe said, waving at the press. 'Just going in to this cage with Gareth the zookeeper, to have a chat with Blossom the lion.

No big deal!'

'Will you be rapping for the lion?' a reporter asked, as there was a loud flurry of cameras flashing.

Inside the cage, Blossom gave a roar at the noise of the camera flashes. The inside of his mouth looked enormous.

'Please don't take photographs, I think you're making Blossom nervous,' Joe said.

He turned to Gareth. 'When exactly was Blossom last fed?'

'Um. What day is it today?' Gareth asked.

'Wednesday,' Joe said.

'I want to say . . . Sunday?' Gareth shrugged. 'Now listen, Joe. This is very important safety information when it comes to how you approach Blossom.'

'Right. Good,' said Joe. 'Fire away!'

'Always look right into his eyes as you walk towards him!'

'Righto.'

'Or is it *never* look right into his eyes?' Gareth frowned. 'It's either always or never, one of the two.'

'That's super helpful,' Joe said, through gritted teeth, as the zookeeper unlocked the cage door and pushed him in.

For the first time, Joe was face to face with Blossom, the snarling, dribbling, badly-named killing machine. Joe opted to keep his eyes closed. That way he couldn't get it wrong.

'Hello pussycat,' he simpered. 'You want some steak? It's very tasty. Much tastier than me.'

'WHHHHHHHHACHOOOOOOOO!' Outside the cage, Jenkins sneezed loudly again, throwing the rest of his coffee over a photographer, who yelped and leapt up in the air before falling into another photographer. Within seconds, there was clattering and yelling and flashing all going on at once.

'No sudden noises. That I do remember,' Gareth said through the bars at Joe.

'I can't stop sneezing . . . achooOOOoooOO-OooOoooo!' Jenkins boomed, making Joe jump with fright and the steak fly out of his hands, landing right on Blossom's face. There was an indignant rumble, followed by a growl, which then became a deafening ROOOOOOOAAAAAR.

But, rather alarmingly, it *didn't* come from Blossom.

'Oh dear,' said Gareth. 'RUN! BLOSSOM'S MUM IS WAKING UP!'

'She's still alive?!'

'Yeah, she's in there somewhere,' Gareth screamed.

'YOU REALLY ARE BAD AT ZOOKEEPING!' Joe cried out, trying to open the cage door. 'It's locked! Why is it locked?'

'Get him out of there!' Violetta shouted.

'It's locked to keep the lions inside. They're really dangerous, you know!' Gareth yelled.

'I thought you said that was just bad press,' Joe yelled back.

'Now, where did I put the key?' Gareth said, pulling out a ring that had about one hundred keys on it.

Joe looked behind him to see Blossom shaking the steak off his head and rubbing his paw on the ground, like he was getting ready to charge the two of them. Mummy Blossom was stalking out behind him.

'FOUND IT! IT WAS IN MY TOP POCKET ALL ALONG!' Gareth screamed, quickly opening the door. Joe scrambled out and slammed the door shut behind him, just as Blossom and Mummy Blossom leapt towards them, crashing against the thick metal bars.

'Oh boy. The press are going love this!' Joe said as he calmed down on the campaign bus later that day.

'Now, listen.' Jim was engaged in a heated phone call. 'You do it my way or you'll never get any access to anything the Prime Minister does again. That includes when he wins! The Prime Minister didn't nearly get eaten by a lion. What he did was save a man from being eaten by a lion. Spin the story round, or you'll never work in TV again,' Jim snapped, hanging up the phone.

Joe sighed and put on the TV.

'The Prime Minister saved the day today when he wrestled a lion to the ground, preventing it from attacking a crowd of his supporters!' The Channel 10 flying studio-copter, or whatever it was called, showed Joe grabbing Gareth and pulling him through the cage like a hero. 'Here's the moment when the Prime Minister's top advisor, Aubrey Fabian Wilbur Jenkins, sneezed and threw hot coffee all over one of our cameramen. The moment that triggered the whole event. Leader of the opposition, Theodore Flunk, has called on Joe Perkins to stop harassing wild beasts . . .'

'O to the M to the G!' Joe smiled. 'Jim, you did it, you re-wrote history!'

'I'm not too happy about them hanging old Jenkins out to dry,' Jim said. 'That was unnecessary.'

'Your first name is *Aubrey*?' Ajay looked at Jenkins, who was dabbing at his red nose.

'You really should have mentioned you were allergic to cats, Jenkins,' Violetta said.

'I didn't think that cats and lions were related. I mean, I know a lion is a sort of a big cat, but I didn't think that being allergic to cats would mean that I'm allergic to lions, too. Frankly, until today, I'd never been near enough to a lion to find out.' Jenkins looked apologetically at Joe. 'Sorry you nearly got eaten, Sir.'

'Whatever. Can we go home now?' Joe asked. 'My heart is still beating like a drum!'

'Home?' Jim shook his head. 'No, we're not going home. Today could have gone better, but we just have to work twice as hard from now on.'

'Just the beginning?' Joe threw a towel over his head and groaned.

'Then I fear you must go on without me, Joe,' Jenkins said, tearfully. 'Sir, after today, it is clear that I am a liability, and therefore would like to hand in my notice.'

SAY HELLO,
WAVE GOODBYE

'I haven't been nibbled or anything, you don't need to resign.'

'It's not just that . . .' Jenkins said. 'Sir, could I have a word, in private?'

'Of course. Jim, does this bus have a quiet, private room we could use?'

'Up the stairs, past the games room, the library, and swimming pool, and you'll see a door marked Private Quiet Room,' Jim said, pointing the way.

A ten-minute walk later—it was a very big bus— Joe and Jenkins were alone.

'Jenkins, you can't go, I need you!' Joe pleaded.

'Sir, you don't need me. You can do this on your own. Listen, other than my grave doubts about Jim Jones, and the fact that I nearly got you killed today, Jim and I are from very different worlds. His is the new world, and well, I feel like it's not my world anymore. I can't keep up with all these constant gadgets and technology, not to mention the robots . . . I think it's time for me to step aside,' Jenkins sighed.

'But Jim isn't here to replace you. You're my personal secretary, not my chief advisor. There's a role for both of you,' Joe protested.

'I know, Sir, but no one wants to be the one who outstays their welcome,' Jenkins smiled sadly.

'But what will you do?' Joe asked.

'Well, I always fancied opening a bow-tie and top-hat shop somewhere in the country. Nothing fancy, just a little place where a gentleman could smarten his look up.' Jenkins smiled, his eyes glazing over as he went off into a daydream. 'I'd call it . . . "Jenkins"'!'

'Good name,' Joe smiled. 'If you're absolutely

sure? Let's go and tell the others, perhaps we could have a bit of a send-off?'

'Thank you, Sir, but if it's OK, I noticed a discreet door just back there, I could nip off and collect my things from Downing Street. I don't want a fuss.'

'Of course,' Joe nodded, tears springing to his eyes.

'It's been an honour and a pleasure to serve you, Sir. Stay true to yourself and—'

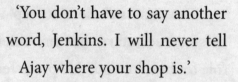

'You don't have to say another word, Jenkins. I will never tell Ajay where your shop is.'

'Thank you. It's just he'd just come and try on all the hats and not buy anything.'

'I know, I know.' Joe saluted his friend, before going in for a big hug.

Joe waved at Jenkins through the window as the bus drove off, and then, feeling sad, he strolled back to the living quarters.

'Where's Jenkins?' Jim asked.

'He's gone, it's time for him to move on,' Joe said.

'You've killed him?!' Ajay cried. 'I'm not sure which emoji goes with murder.'

'No, he's just decided to retire. It's not because of the sneezing thing, either. Jenkins felt the time had come to hand in his notice,' Joe said.

Violetta and Jim looked at each other.

'Well, I'll miss the old boy,' Jim said, quickly. 'Violetta, shall we go and find a bottle of pop? Perhaps we could toast Jenkins' departure, Joe?'

'Yes, that would be nice,' Joe said, sadly.

In the kitchen area, Jim and Violetta rummaged around for some soft drinks.

'Good work,' Violetta whispered.

'Well, a man with such unfortunate allergies to cats was always going to suffer so close to lions. Thank goodness for Ajay's Instagram feed,' Jim said, winking.

'Still, I didn't think it would be this easy to get rid of him,' Violetta said.

'People like Jenkins need a sword to fall on, they need a noble way out. That's what we gave him. One down, one to go . . .' he added, looking back at Ajay, who was picking his nose.

'*He's* going to be a little more difficult to get rid of, I think?' said Violetta. 'I suspect Ajay is as stubborn as a verruca.'

'We don't get rid of him directly,' Jim said. 'We just need to sow the seeds of treachery. We need to get Ajay to switch his loyalty from Joe Perkins to us . . .' Jim beamed as he found what he'd been looking for. 'Aha!' He pulled out a bottle of cherry cola. '1996. A wonderful vintage. Let's go and toast the demise—I mean the departure—of dear, old Jenkins.'

NEW MAN

'Hello ... well ... I'm still here, still flying around ... in the air, bumping about ...' Charlie James said, high up in the heli-telly-studio. 'Funny story, I didn't realize how travel sick I can get. Flying has never made me ill before, but then again, I haven't flown non-stop for nearly a week before ... Can I get an iced water please?'

Charlie wiped the sweat off his pale and clammy forehead. 'So today's a big day, because the Prime Minister is finally launching his Green Space initiative. Apparently, he will be parachuting in ... God, I wish I had a parachute. At least then I could jump out of this flying torture-chamber.'

'Parachuting?!' Joe said.

'Yes!' Ajay said. 'It's perfect. I've run the data and you arriving by parachute will make you 0.234% more popular. Although there is a 4.557393% chance that your parachute won't open and you'll go splat. But on the plus side, if you do perish, you'll be a hero and your approval rating will go through the roof . . .'

'Stop talking,' Joe said, trying to wake up. 'I'm so tired.'

'Sleep badly?' Ajay asked.

'Yes, it's this new regime,' Joe said. 'I mean, do I really have to sleep hanging upside down? What's wrong with beds?'

Ajay ignored Joe and tapped his headset. 'Big Bird on the move. Joe should be with you in T-minus twelve seconds, Jim.'

'You're really taking this apprenticeship with Jim very seriously, aren't you?' Joe said. 'And what are you wearing? Have you been through the

Makeover 3000?'

'No. Well, yes. But I promise I was just looking for the loo, and I may have wandered in accidentally, and this is what happened.' He gestured to his clothes. 'I definitely, DEFINITELY, didn't intend them to make me look like Jim.'

'Hmmm.'

'Listen, when a man like Jim takes you under his wing, you have to shape up or ship out!'

'I've just never seen you do much on your iPad except look at people falling over on YouTube'

'That was the old Ajay. That Ajay is gone. I have been reborn, Joe. I'm part of the digital matrix— the machine that will get you elected. Now, stop wasting time and get going.'

Ajay tapped his ear-piece again. 'Can we get Big Bird the rejuvenation smoothie, please? And extra ginger. It looks like his

yin may need reconnecting with his yang.'

'Well my yin might be more reconnected with my yang if I hadn't had to sleep upside down,' Joe said.

'Sleeping upside down can increase blood flow to your brain. It means you are sharper, quicker—it's all about increasing your percentage points. A 1% here and there makes you a better human being and a better person.' Ajay showed Joe an animation on his iPad.

'Incredible,' Joe muttered, throwing on some clothes.

'Isn't it? This is Jim's programme, he built this model from scratch.'

'No, I mean your iPad doesn't even have a single gaming app on it. No YouTube and no games!' Joe smiled at last and took a deep breath. 'Right, what's for breakfast? I'm in the mood for bacon and waffles, maybe both, definitely both.'

'You haven't got time,' said Ajay. 'I've ordered you a smoothie.'

'What?'

'If you're building a Ferrari you need to make sure the fuel is top notch, you can't run on bacon and waffles,' Ajay said.

'Is that a . . .?' Joe asked, peering closely at his friend's face.

'What? I think a moustache like Jim's looks great,' Ajay said, blushing.

'How did you grow a moustache overnight?' Joe asked suspiciously.

'HAS ANYONE SEEN MY FALSE EYELASHES?' Violetta shouted from down the other end of the bus.

'Oh, I see,' Joe smiled.

'Listen, don't say a word,' Ajay pleaded. 'I think it makes me look more sophisticated . . . ARGH! We're nearly fourteen seconds late! Come on, it's time for the breakfast meeting.'

Ajay ushered Joe out of his sleeping quarters and through to the main room of the bus, where Team Joe had their daily meeting and talked about the day's itinerary.

'Big Bird on the move. Big Bird sitting down. The eagle has landed!' Ajay shrieked into his earpiece.

'Yes, I can see that, Ajay, thanks,' said Jim, who had a pile of papers on his lap. 'Right. Where to begin?'

'May I?' Ajay said.

'Er, sure,' Jim smiled.

'Well, the numbers . . .' Ajay started.

'Ooh, sorry I'm late,' Violetta said, bustling into the room. 'I couldn't find my false eyelashes anywhere.'

'As I was saying,' Ajay said, putting one hand over his top lip to cover the false moustache. 'The numbers have come through and we are now ahead of Theodore Flunk. We are polling about three points ahead, nationally, which will put Flunk bottom . . .'

'AHAHA!' Joe laughed, 'Flunk's bottom!'

'Please Joe, grow up.' Ajay shook his head. 'It will put Theodore behind, with us winning the election. These are just some early numbers I've been working on, but the projections are looking good. We just have to keep on driving home that core message.' Ajay paused. 'I believe you have some thoughts on that Jim.'

'Thank you, Ajay. I really think the parachute launch will play well with the voters. I think we will see you surge into the lead position. In fact,' Jim said, looking at his watch, 'you need to get ready. The helicopter will be here any moment. Ajay and I will finish off the speech.'

'Oh, right, I'd best get into a suit,' Joe said, wandering off to the Makeover 3000, reluctantly.

'Don't forget to ask for a parachute!' Ajay yelled after him. 'I feel that might be important!'

'Right, so the speech,' Ajay unlocked his iPad. 'I've been working on the Why Parks Are Brilliant bit.'

'Yeah, there's been a bit of a change of plan, Ajay,' Violetta said.

'Oh, really?' Ajay said.

'Yes, we ran the numbers through the computers and well, the park thing isn't going to work for us,' said Jim.

'Oh, I thought people really liked the idea. Who doesn't like parks?' Ajay said.

'Well, builders for one,' said Violetta.

'Builders?' Ajay asked.

'Yes. I mean that space could be used for building things. Important things. It's something you might struggle to understand now but you'll get it when you're older.'

'I hadn't thought of that,' said Ajay, looking unsure.

'All we're doing is going by what the computer stats tell us. You do trust the computers, don't you, Ajay?'

'Always!' Ajay said, enthusiastically.

'Good. So that's why we've dropped the Green Space initiative. Instead of cluttering this city up with damp old parks, the stats tell us that we should build more stuff that we can then sell. And then we could use that money to buy things—'

'Like hospitals?' Ajay asked.

'Maybe. Or perhaps we could turn Big Ben into an Apple Watch . . .'

'Ooh, that would be cool,' Ajay said, then frowned. 'But Joe loves parks, they're his thing. Are you saying he's changed his mind? I mean, it doesn't seem like the sort of thing he'd do. An Apple Watch would be amazing, but I think he would prefer parks. Let me go and talk to him.'

'NO!' Violetta and Jim cried together.

'Look, Joe's totally on board. He just wants to win. You want him to win too, don't you?' Jim asked.

'Yes, of course I do,' Ajay said.

'So you'd better change his speech.' Jim handed him a bit of paper. 'Here you go, here's all you need to know about the new plan.'

Violetta leaned forward and looked closely at Ajay's face. 'Are those my eyelashes?'

THE SIZE OF A COW

'Can you just stop and ask for directions, Johnson!' Theodore Flunk snapped.

'It's fine, I know where we're going,' Johnson said, trying to read the map and steer at the same time.

'This is the worst election bus ever. In fact, it's not even a proper bus, it's an old transit van you bought off the web.'

'Nonsense, Sir,' Johnson said. 'This is the finest engineering you can buy for under £150. It's not let us down yet, apart from that one time when the wheel fell off.'

'Oh great. We're driving around in a clapped-out old motor and Perkins' bus has a swimming pool, a five-star chef on board, and a posh coffee machine.'

'We have a coffee machine, Sir.' Johnson looked out at the road signs. 'Is this the A38, or B532?'

'We have a machine that gives you coffee or chicken soup,' said Flunk. 'That means that every cup of coffee tastes of chicken and every cup of soup tastes of coffee.'

'It's fusion cooking, and all the rage.' Johnson was looking stressed. 'Is this one-way?'

'Joe Perkins' bus also has satellite navigation,' Flunk said. 'I mean, who's ever heard of an election battlebus getting lost! We have an event in half an hour, I'm supposed to be giving a speech to hundreds of my supporters and we don't know where we're going. Joe is beating us in every way and what are we doing about it?'

'We have the newspapers. Well, one journalist, on our side,' Johnson said. 'That was my idea, remember, you said it was a good one.'

'Yes, the trouble is, Joe Perkins' team is always one

step ahead of us. By the time the newspaper comes out, his team has put out a video, or done a funny Facebook post. I am currently being outsmarted by a thirteen-year-old.' Theodore snapped. 'Take a right here.'

'We need to rethink our strategy. We're only a few days out. In order to catch Joe Perkins, we need to *think* like Joe Perkins.' Theodore narrowed his eyes. 'Where are we? Oh, this is not good!'

'I don't think this is the right way,' Johnson said. 'Unless we're doing a rally to a bunch of cows. Can cows charge?' Johnson asked.

'Yes, they can be very dangerous. They're famously dangerous!' Theodore yelled, 'Get us out of here.'

'Oh,' Johnson said. 'Well, this is awkward, we're stuck in the mud, going nowhere. I think we need a push?' Johnson turned to his boss and gave him a tentative smile.

'I am running to be Prime Minister of this country, I am not going to get out and push a tin can on wheels out of a muddy field while a herd of cows charges at me. It wouldn't look good.'

'There's no one here. Well, apart from those ramblers.' Johnson pointed at two people wearing fleeces.

'Perfect!' Flunk smiled. 'They should have a map and a compass between them. They must know their way around these parts. Where's my megaphone?' He rummaged around the back seat of the bus. 'Aha! Open a window.'

'Yes, Sir.'

'Hello there!' called Flunk, jovially. 'Any chance of a hand? We're a bit lost.'

The ramblers, a hearty-looking man and woman, walked over to the bus and peered through the window.

'Hello, there,' the man said.

'Hello, I'm—' Theodore started.

'Roger,' the woman cut in. 'That's Theodore Flunk. He's campaigning to be Prime Minister. You know, him from the TV.'

'I know who he is, Susan,' Roger said, removing his bobble hat. 'What are you doing parked in a field of cows? You can't be that desperate for votes?' He laughed. 'See what I did there Susan, I did a funny.'

'Oh, put a sock in it, Roger,' Susan groaned. 'Tell me, Mr Flunk, when are you going to do something about the potholes in the roads?'

'It will be my top priority,' said Flunk. 'Anyway, we're a bit lost. We're supposed to be going to a rally in a place called . . .'

'Little Bibbington,' Johnson said, pointing at the map.

'Oh, you're not in the right place, at all,' Roger said, shaking his head.

'Yes, we were getting that impression.' Theodore's smile was forced as he tried not to lose his patience.

'Well. You want to turn round, head left, then right, then second left for half a mile . . .' Susan started.

'Hey, would you two like to come to the rally? We can discuss the pothole issue on the way?' Theodore suggested.

'Well, I suppose we could, why not?' Roger said. 'Is this a new thing then, giving lifts is the new canvassing?'

'Sort of, yes,' Theodore smiled. 'You can have a

backstage peek at how a political campaign is run. We also have the latest in . . . er, fusion cooking on board the bus. And then you can direct us to Little Bibbington.'

'Can we bring our dog?' Roger asked.

'Oh gosh, is that a dog?' Theodore said, peering out of the window. 'I thought it was just a pile of mud!'

'No, that's old Bill. He's very old but we love him dearly, despite his leaky bottom and terrible breath,' Susan said.

'Er . . . well, the more the merrier,' Theodore said uneasily. 'All supporters and their pets are welcome.' He smiled. 'I couldn't ask a small favour first, though?'

'What is it?' Susan asked.

'How fit are you?' Theodore said, looking at the stuck wheels. 'Fancy giving us a push?'

'You hold onto the dog, Roger,' Susan said, rolling up her sleeves. 'Your bus is only small, not like that Joe Perkins' with his big space-age thing.'

'Oh, yes,' Roger joined in. 'Perkins' bus is very sleek and modern, isn't it? Not my cup of tea, but talk about professional! You could do with a bit of that, Mr Flunk. I read that Perkins has his best friend on the campaign team. Ajay. They've started calling him the "Mini Rottweiler".' Roger held out his phone. 'Look, there he is, next to Joe, about to make his speech. It's a shame he got there before you.'

Theodore snatched the phone out of his hand.

'Hmmm. The "Mini Rottweiler", you say?' Theodore's eyes widened, as an idea popped into his head. A cunning, rather sneaky idea. 'Ajay Patel has certainly transformed his image. I always thought he was a bit gormless. Clearly, there was more to him than met the eye!'

'Yeah, but who needs Ajay when you've got me?' said Johnson, laughing nervously.

'Exactly,' Theodore smiled. 'Listen, take a left here, I need to make a quick detour . . .'

'RIGHT, PRIME MINISTER. ONCE YOU JUMP OUT OF THE HELICOPTER, YOU COUNT TO THREE AND PULL THIS CHORD!' Mark, the parachute instructor yelled above the roar of the whooshing blades. 'HAVE YOU EVER PARA-CHUTED BEFORE?'

'NO!' Joe yelled back. 'I'M A KID, OF COURSE I HAVEN'T!'

'IT'S JUST LIKE RIDING A BIKE,' the instructor, who had enormous shoulders and a chin to match, told him.

'NO, IT ISN'T!' Joe insisted.

'YOU'LL BE FINE, I HAVEN'T LOST ANY OF MY TRAINEES YET!' Mark yelled. 'READY?'

'NO, NOT REALLY!' Joe cried, as white as a sheet.

'GREAT!' Without further ado, Mark opened the door and pushed him out of the helicopter. It seemed to Joe that this was almost certainly against the law. I mean, you can't go around pushing Prime Ministers out of helicopters, can you? But the rights and wrongs of it would have to wait because Joe had some important screaming to get on with.

'WHAAAAAAAAAAAAAAAAAAAAAA!'

he wailed, falling fast. 'ONE . . . TWO . . . THREE!'
Joe pulled the chord on his backpack just in time.

Instantly, the parachute ballooned out and the roaring stopped. Joe was floating in the air, drifting left and right and down, like a feather falling to the ground. It was the best sensation ever.

'WHA-HEY, I LOVE THIS!' he shouted. 'I AM SOOOOOOO DOING THIS AGAIN.'

He waved as best he could to the crowd watching him from the ground. Still clinging to the parachute jump ropes, he pulled and tugged, left and right, the way Mark had instructed him to steer. Below him, the campaign bus had arrived, and he could just about make out Ajay, Jim, and Alice—waving and grinning like mad—and there was another minibus, which looked a lot like Theodore Flunk's campaign bus, parked a few streets away. Weird.

Joe floated down slowly, well slowly-ish, because it suddenly felt as though he was coming in quite quickly. He grabbed the two ropes and pulled them down as best he could.

'WHAAAAAAAAAAAAAA!' He landed with a thud, the parachute draping itself over him like a blanket as he wriggled around underneath it. For a second, no one said anything; there was just silence and a few worried gasps before Joe burst through the parachute.

'HELLO!' he said. 'I'M A-OK!' he said, giving the thumbs up.

'Nice one, Joe!' Ajay cheered.

'Thank you!' Joe said, taking off the backpack.

'So, your speech is in the teleprompter by the podium,' Ajay said, prepping Joe before his big moment.

'Oh, OK, I was just going to ad-lib, be more spontaneous,' said Joe. 'You know, keep it real.'

'Are you sure?' Ajay asked.

'Erm . . .' Joe said, uncertainly. 'Actually, Jim knows best,' said Joe. 'Some of his ideas are a bit far-fetched but he's really come through for me.' Joe waved at Alice and smiled. 'So, I just read exactly what it says on the teleprompter?'

'Yep,' Ajay said.

'Good crowd,' Joe said.

'Totally. Very supportive!' Ajay said proudly. 'Mind you, they're not doing it for free.'

'What do you mean? You're *paying* people to turn up?! How do we know what, you know, real people think?'

'The stats from the computer?' Ajay shrugged.

Just then, Violetta and Jim came marching towards them.

'Good work with the numbers, Ajay!' she said.

'Thanks, lovely.' Ajay said.

'Lovely?' whispered Joe. 'I thought you hated Violetta?'

'She's not that bad. We're actually very similar in our brainpower,' said Ajay. 'When we put our heads together, we're like one giant superbrain.'

'If you say so,' Joe shook his head.

'Ajay, I want you to have this. You've earned it.' Violetta slapped a spare false eyelash on Ajay's top lip. 'I'm going to have to put a sticker on the real Jim so I can tell you two apart.'

'Yeah, it is getting difficult to tell who's who round here,' Joe muttered.

'Well, for future reference, Joe, Jim's in his fifties and five feet nine inches tall, and I'm a small Asian boy!' Ajay joked. 'But enough of the lols. Let's get back to business. You need to go out there and breathe life into my speech!'

'You wrote the whole thing?' Joe asked.

'Yeah, but I couldn't have done it without Jim and Violetta's data.'

'Nonsense, Ajay. This was all your own work,' Violetta said. 'We can't take credit for your ideas.'

'You guys!' Ajay blushed before noticing the time. 'Oh, my, we're three and half seconds late,' he said, shoving Joe forward. 'Just read from the screen, Joe. Don't change a single word. Each word was hand-picked so that people would find your speech as pleasing as possible.'

'Righto,' said Joe, noticing Alice in the crowd, smiling and pushing forward towards him.

'Hello, Prime Minister,' she said. 'I've been really looking forward to today!'

'Me too!' Joe said, looking around the derelict space around them. 'Wow, it's so much worse in real life. Listen, we've got some JCBs round the corner that will tidy this up in no time. They'll come in after I've finished my speech, so the cameras get to see it all.'

'Brilliant,' said Alice, beaming.

'Are we all set?' Jim asked Violetta quietly, as they stood a short distance from Joe and Alice, near the stage.

'Yep, as soon as the speech is done, the diggers will get busy on the first stage of turning all this into an office block,' Violetta whispered. 'Then we move to the next phase of the plan.'

Ajay, meanwhile, was eagerly waiting by the other side of the stage.

'Pssst.'

Ajay turned, but there was no one there. 'Hello?' he said, looking around while Joe started addressing the crowd.

'Over here.' The voice seemed to be coming from a nearby bush and Ajay walked over slowly.

'You're getting warmer.'

'I'm getting more scared,' Ajay said, holding his iPad up as a shield.

'That's it. I'm here, in the bush,' the voice continued, and then a body shot out of the foliage. It looked like a scrawny old woman wearing a headscarf.

'AAARGH!' Ajay jumped in fright. 'Who are you, and what do you want from me?'

'It's me!' and the 'lady' ripped off her headscarf to reveal a familiar balding, bony head.

'Theodore Flunk?' Ajay frowned. 'What on earth are *you* doing here? You know you could have just watched all this on the telly, right?'

'But I want to talk to you, Ajay,' Theodore said.

'Well, I don't want to talk to you. You're our rival. If Jim Jones sees me associating with you, I'll be fired. I'll be done. I'll be sourdough toast!'

'Oh, just get in here!' Theodore said impatiently, pulling Ajay head first into the bush.

'Unhand me, you ruffian!' Ajay protested. 'You can't go around pulling people into bushes.' He looked down at his clothes. 'Oh, great, I've got sap on my suit.'

'Listen,' Theodore said urgently. 'Come and join Team Flunk.'

'You what?' Ajay said, shocked.

'You heard. Come and work for me. You're just what I need to win.'

Ajay shook his head. 'Nope, can't do that.'

'Look,' said Theodore. 'Sure, I want to win, and for that I need the best of the best. But I'm thinking of advancing your career prospects, too, Ajay. Word on the street is that you're known as the "Mini Rottweiler", and that you're even more ruthless than Jim Jones. The apprentice has become the sorcerer!'

'Cool. I don't really know what that means, but it sounds awesome,' Ajay smiled.

'You're bigger than Joe now, Ajay. You need to work with someone who really appreciates your amazing political brainpower.'

'Are you talking to me?' Ajay said, glancing over his shoulder.

'Yes, I'm talking to you! You're a winner and I need winners. I mean, does Joe really buy into your ideas, or is he always trying to hold you back? Treating you like you're the sidekick in the relationship. Do you really want to stay the Watson to his Sherlock?'

'Erm,' Ajay scratched his head. 'When you put it like that . . . I mean, Joe wouldn't even be Prime Minister if it wasn't for me.'

'Really? How's that?' Theodore leaned in closer.

'Well. He didn't know whether he should become

Prime Minister at all at first, and so, do you know what I did?'

'What? What great advice or strategy did you come up with?'

'I said he should go for it! And he did.'

'Well, sometimes the best strategies are the simplest strategies,' Theodore said. 'And no one's simpler than you, Ajay. Come on, join my team. I guarantee you the top job when we win. Personal advisor to me, the new Prime Minister.'

'Yeah. I could be the new Jenkins!' Ajay said. 'But a really cool version.'

'YES!' Theodore grinned. 'Now you're getting it!'

'Wait...' Ajay frowned. 'No. Joe is my best friend. He treasures my advice. He'd be lost without me. I can't desert him in his hour of need.'

'It's time to think about your future, Ajay.' Theodore took a card out of his pocket. 'Listen, here's my number, give me a call.'

'Hmmm.'

'And I should add,' said Flunk, 'that I will pay you handsomely.'

Ajay's eyes lit up. 'How handsomely?'

'Name your price.'

'Erm . . .' Ajay thought of the biggest number he could imagine. 'Seven?'

'Seven hundred thousand it is—if you can win me this election.'

'SEVEN HUNDRED THOUSAND!' Ajay shrieked. 'But . . . I can't . . . I won't . . . Let me take that card.' He grabbed Flunk's card and shoved it into his pocket.

'Call me,' said Theodore, before retreating mysteriously into the bush and out of sight.

Ajay wriggled out of the bush and looked over to the stage to see that Joe was about to begin. Joe was his best and oldest friend. But Ajay couldn't help thinking of all the games he could buy with seven hundred thousand pounds. How many milkshakes. How many packets of cheese strings . . . !

GET UP, STAND UP

'Please welcome to the stage, Joe Perkins!' boomed Jim Jones's voice.

Joe walked onstage waving to the cheering crowd, and wondering inside how many of them had been paid to be there.

'HELLO EVERYONE!' Joe scanned the teleprompter, determined to stick to the script exactly. 'It's so great to be here, to talk about Green Space. We all love green spaces, they're a brilliant idea, but . . .' Joe squinted at the words coming through. 'Sometimes politicians have to make difficult decisions and occasionally completely change their minds—?'

Joe stopped, frowning. 'Erm . . . sometimes you have to take something like the Green Space initiative and reconsider it. I mean, who needs parks, anyway . . . Erm, I need parks . . . ?' he added, off-message. Then Joe looked over at Violetta, whose eyes were wide with what looked like shock, and then to Ajay, who mouthed, 'TRUST ME—JUST READ IT!'

Joe felt he had no choice. He no longer trusted himself to make it up on the spot. Look how badly the rapping at the old people's home went down with the newspapers. Either he was going to have to stop the speech all together, or read it word for word, even though he was saying things he didn't believe in. Joe coughed, buying some time. Ajay was his best mate. There was no way he'd stitch Joe up. There must be a reason for this. Maybe it would get better by the end?

Joe smiled at the audience and met Jim's eye. Just like Violetta, Jim's usually jovial expression had turned a bit sour. I mean, if looks could kill, Joe might be dead already. They'd trusted Ajay to take care of the speech and for Joe to read it, and now it was Joe who was letting them all down. He had to trust that they knew best.

'I mean,' Joe continued, 'who needs parks? No one really. If we want to play football, we can just play FIFA. If we want to see some nature, well that's what those Netflix documentaries are for, right? No. I say it's time to get rid of this wasteland. Sell it off and use the money for other, important things.'

The crowd fell deadly silent.

'Erm . . . so, I hereby rename the Green Space initiative "OPERATION BUILD, BUILD, BUILD"!'

The crowd booed and hissed. This wasn't supposed to happen! Didn't we pay them to be here? thought Joe frantically. He didn't even believe in that speech— he only said it because he thought Jim knew best.

'What have I done?' Joe whispered, as he finally locked eyes with Alice. Unlike everyone else, Alice wasn't booing but she didn't look angry either. She had the most disappointed and sad expression that Joe had ever seen.

Joe marched off stage and crashed straight into Ajay. 'What the heck was that?' he said. '"Operation Build, Build, Build"?'

'It's what the opinion polls said they all wanted to hear,' said Ajay.

'Ajay, you wrote things in that speech you know I don't believe! Now, get out of my way. I have to go and try and fix things with Alice.'

'But . . . this is what you wanted, bro . . .' Ajay stuttered, as Joe stormed off.

'Don't worry, Ajay,' Violetta said, sidling up next to him out of nowhere, 'they're never grateful, these politicians. They always turn into terrible divas. Why don't you let Jim take you for a nice ginger smoothie?'

'Joe was really mean,' Ajay said petulantly. 'I think we've grown apart.'

'It happens to the best of us . . .' Violetta soothed, looking over Ajay's head and subtly winking at Jim Jones.

THE STATE I'M IN

'I'm so sorry, Joe, I had no idea Ajay had written all that!' Violetta banged on the campaign bus door. 'Please let me in!' We need to talk this disaster through! How could he do that to you?!'

She waited, until slowly the door crept opened and Joe appeared in his pyjamas. His hair was sticking up everywhere like a well-used loo brush and he had a few doughnut crumbs round his mouth.

'Oh, dear.' Violetta patted him awkwardly on the shoulder. 'Don't be sad, Joe. You're still winning. I mean, you've got the public on your side, judging by the reaction to Ajay's traitorous speech.'

'How can that be possible? And even if I am still ahead in the polls, why do I feel so miserable?' Joe said.

'Well, life at the top isn't easy. There are always sacrifices to make. And there will always be some people who don't have your best interests at heart. People you trusted but who want to take you down. And then you have to let them go . . .' She crooked her head to the side. 'It's all part and parcel of being a great leader, Joe . . .'

'Don't worry Ajay, it's not your fault, I thought your speech was great,' Jim said, pouring Ajay a glass of Ribena. 'You can't please everyone, you know. And we're all here to help Joe win the votes, aren't we?'

Ajay looked doubtful. 'I mean, I was only going on the data you sent me from the computer,' he said. 'You know, the stuff that said giant high-rise office blocks were way more popular than trees and grass and flowers and fresh air.' He sighed. 'I thought Joe was on board with the message, but maybe we can change it back to what he wanted?'

Jim shook his head. 'I think it's too late, Ajay. I think Joe appearing to change his mind again would look indecisive and weak. I think we have to go forward with Operation Build, Build, Build.'

'But Joe's my best friend,' said Ajay. 'And best friends always have each other's backs.'

Jim put his chin in his hand, thoughtfully, and Ajay noticed that his eyes looked a bit teary.

'What?' Ajay said. 'What's the matter, Jim?'

'Man, this is hard.' Jim shook his head. 'I hate being the bearer of bad news.'

Ajay slumped in his seat and waited for the worst.

'I don't think Joe's going to come round on this,' said Jim. 'I overheard him talking to Violetta. The things he was saying about you—whoa. He's boiling with rage.'

Ajay's lip wobbled. 'What things?' he said, in a tiny voice. 'Really, really mean things?'

Jim nodded seriously. 'I'm afraid so. Things I can't even repeat.'

'What shall I do?'

'I'm really sorry, kid. I think the only way out of this for you, is for you to resign.'

'RESIGN!'

'Make a stand. You're never going to win back Joe's friendship, and this way you'll leave his campaign team with dignity, knowing that you, Ajay, did everything you could. That you wrote the speech that will win him this election—even if he is ungrateful and doesn't appreciate it. It's time for you to do your own thing, kid. Do you want to be forever known as "Joe's ex-best friend Ajay"? The Garfunkel to his Simon, the Dec to his Ant. Maybe it's time to reinvent Ajay as a solo artist, as it were . . .'

Ajay sniffed. 'Sounds like I don't have much choice if Joe doesn't want me around anymore,' he said.

'There, there.' Violetta took away Joe's plate, scraped clean of the huge portion of beans on toast he'd just eaten. 'Feeling better?'

'Not really,' Joe shrugged. 'I'm just angry with

myself. And Alice heard me say all that stuff I don't believe in. We can change our minds, though, can't we? We can go back to the Green Space initiative?'

Violetta smiled tightly. 'Of course ... except, well, it's something that Jim keeps saying.' She paused. 'Changing your mind looks weak and indecisive. I hate to say it, but unfortunately I think we're stuck with this new idea now. Otherwise the papers will take you to task. As will Flunk. You will be an utter laughing stock.'

'Oh,' Joe sighed.

'But at least Ajay has offered to resign,' she said quickly, picking up her mug and taking a sip.

'RESIGN!' Joe cried, 'AJAY WANTS TO RESIGN?!'

'Well, he's clearly very hurt after your big argument. Apparently, he doesn't think you'll ever be able to work together again. Personally, I think he's deeply ambitious. He's always been jealous of your role. I wouldn't be surprised if that whole speech he wrote was an act of sabotage ...' she sighed.

'But he's my best mate ...' Joe said, getting up and

going to the window. 'You really think he planned any of this?'

'It's just a theory. Nothing to get worked up about, Joe.'

He frowned, pulling the curtains all the way open. He heard a door slam, then Jim and Ajay appeared round the side of the bus. They must have been at the other end all the time and now Ajay had stormed out of the back exit in a right mood.

'I can't believe this!' Joe heard Ajay snap at Jim. 'I can't believe it's come to this, but if that's what he wants, then fine! I have other people who want me. Other people who value my skillz!'

'What are you going to do now?' Jim asked. 'Are you going to go and pack your bags and leave?'

Ajay shrugged. 'I'm not a coward, Jim. I'll say goodbye first.' With that, Ajay started marching back over to the bus.

'He's coming!' Joe said, panicking. 'What do I say?'

'Just be stern and thank him for his service. Don't

be emotional,' Violetta advised. 'It's not professional.'

'So that's it, is it?' Joe said calmly, as Ajay appeared in the doorway. 'You're off?'

'Looks like it, bro,' Ajay shrugged. 'Time for pastures new and all that. Time for new opportunities.'

'I see,' said Joe. 'You're *really* resigning?'

'Yup,' said Ajay. 'I mean, I did my best, Joe, I really did.'

'Yes, Ajay,' Joe crossed his arms, coldly. 'I know what you did.'

'And what does that mean?' Ajay looked stung.

'Nothing. Nothing at all,' Joe smiled icily.

The door opened and Jim stuck his head inside the bus.

'Look, Joe, we have to get going to the next event. Why don't I stay with Ajay, get him a car back to London, and you and Violetta can go on.'

'Fine by me,' Ajay said.

'And me,' Joe nodded.

'Great. Well . . . cheerio Joe.' Ajay smiled a sad

smile and marched over to Jim in the doorway.

'Oh, Ajay . . .' Joe said.

'What?' Ajay said, turning around with the tiniest glint of what looked like hope in his eyes.

'We're going to need the iPad and earpiece back.'

'And my eyelashes,' Violetta added.

Ajay stared at them, blinking tears from his eyes, before he snapped into recovery mode.

'Fine, fine. ENJOY!' he said, a bit too loudly, taking the iPad and earpiece out of his bag. 'There are a few strategies on the iPad. You're welcome to them, they're useless to me now.'

Ajay handed over his devices and then slowly began peeling Violetta's eyelashes off his top lip.

'Owowowowow!' he moaned. 'OW. OW. OW. OW.'

I THINK I'M ALONE NOW

'So, what do we think? The blue suit or the grey?' Jim asked Violetta.

'Hmmm. The grey is more sophisticated, but the blue fits better. Can we see you in the charcoal again?' Violetta asked Joe.

'I'm tiiiiiiired, and I want to call Alice and figure out a way to put this right.'

'You must concentrate, Joe. You do *want* to keep your job as Prime Minister, don't you?'

'S'pose . . .' Joe mumbled, exhausted.

'Look at me when I'm talking to you,' Violetta demanded.

'Yeah, OK. You know I do,' Joe squirmed, with his hands in his pockets. 'It's just that this job used to be fun.'

'Joe. Listen to your deputy,' Jim said. 'You don't get to be Prime Minister by playing PlayStation, sitting around listening to music, and eating doughnuts. You think Winston Churchill spent his days playing *Fortnite*?'

'But these trousers are so itchy. What's wrong with my old clothes?' Joe asked, scratching his legs.

'You scuffed your old trousers playing football when you should have been practising your walk,' Violetta said.

'I just wanted to play and have fun for five minutes. I've been on this bus for, like, EVER!'

'Now listen, young man. Jim got you this nice bus. This is a special treat for big boy Prime Ministers. Would you rather we went around in Flunk's awful old bus? There's no PlayStation on that. No café to serve you hot drinks and the like.'

'But I never get to go on PlayStation, and the café doesn't even do Nando's, which is, like, the best food ever made, and that's a fact. And why do I need to practise walking? I've been walking for years, and it's never been a problem before,' Joe said, pulling at his tie, which felt like it was strangling him.

Joe looked over at the empty seats where Ajay and Jenkins used to sit. Ajay was an annoying traitor, but at least he was fun. And Jenkins had never made him put on really heavy trousers made of itchy wool. He had good friends. Once.

'We are only a few hours away from the live, televised debate between you and Theodore Flunk. Everything must be perfect, including your walk. It's like when you're trying on a new pair of shoes at the shoe shop and your mum makes you walk needlessly up and down.' Violetta smiled a smile that did not reach her eyes.

'Actually, that is true. I do find it hard not to walk weirdly when I'm trying on shoes.' Joe scratched his head. 'Let me try . . .' He took a deep breath and walked up and down the battlebus. 'OH MY, I CAN'T EVEN WALK NOW, THIS IS A DISASTER!'

Joe slumped down on the sofa. 'We may as well just give up now. I'm not going to win this election. Look!' Joe grabbed an iPad. 'Theodore is catching up!'

Violetta glanced at Jim.

'Look, I didn't want to tell you this, but the day you made your big speech, the one Ajay cunningly wrote, I saw him having a secret meeting in a bush.'

'Excuse me?' Joe frowned. 'Well. Maybe he was just going for a number two? He had been eating a lot of bran, as I remember.'

Violetta pulled out her iPhone. 'I caught it on camera. Do you see who Ajay's talking to? It's Theodore Flunk.'

'NO WAY!' Joe enlarged the picture. 'He wouldn't . . .'

'I'm afraid he would,' she said. 'This is undeniable proof of your so-called best friend stabbing you in the back.' Violetta bit her fist and looked like she was choking back tears.

'I . . . I blame myself . . .' Jim put in. 'I thought making him my second in command would be a good move for him, but it seems it really did go to his head and he went power-crazy. It's all my fault.'

'No, well, come on guys. You weren't to know. And we can still win this.' Joe stood up and grabbed an energy bar from the counter, looking frantic, before plodding mindlessly up and down the bus. 'Look! I'm walking! And it looks mostly normal! What else can we do? Come on, we need to floor Theodore—oh, I like that, it rhymes—maybe we can use that? Now, do we need some more policies? You know, big ideas. Ways to bring people together.'

'Hmmm . . .' Jim said, glancing at Violetta. 'Well, we need something new. Something out of this world'. He walked over to the whiteboard and grabbed a marker pen from his pocket, pulling the lid off with his teeth and spitting it across the floor, before flipping over a huge sheet of paper. OUT OF THIS WORLD, he wrote. 'Now what else do we know that people like?'

'SPACE!' Joe exclaimed. 'I know you said I couldn't go back on cancelling the Green Space initiative but . . . I don't know . . . maybe leave the green bit and keep the space?'

'Quite right!' Jim said, writing SPACE next to OUT OF THIS WORLD. 'Now,' he said. 'What do people want?'

'Erm . . .' Joe was looking frazzled now, still plodding doggedly up and down the bus, with the latest popularity poll clutched in his fist.

'Maybe people want something new?' he asked.

'Yes, they would prefer to move somewhere new. They think that this planet is broken,' Violetta said. 'They wish they could leave.'

LEAVE EARTH, Jim wrote down.

'Wow, when it comes to brainstorming, you really know how to rock it,' said Violetta.

ROCKET, Jim scribbled, then he sat back and stared at the words. 'So, what do we think? Remember there are no wrong or right answers here, it's just a free-form jazz-fest of ideas. Say, don't think!'

'I KNOW, I KNOW!' Joe said, jumping up and down, 'WE COULD ALL MOVE SOMEWHERE NEW . . . BUT WHERE . . .' He gazed out of the battlebus window, fizzing with all these new ideas, desperate to win, and feeling confused.

'I think what you're trying to say is . . . THE PLANET IS BROKEN SO LET'S ALL MOVE TO SPACE!' Jim grinned and sat back. 'Joe, you are a genius.'

'I am?' Joe asked.

'It's inspired, Joe. Your cleverest idea yet.'

'Really?'

'When you announce your brilliant new idea,

they'll be voting for you in their droves. Now let's do a run through of the debate, I have an idea.' Jim raced out of the room and returned a few seconds later with the various devices Ajay had left behind. 'Here, put this in.' Jim thrust an earpiece at Joe. 'Now if I can just connect it to this . . .' he said, pairing it up with his smartphone. 'Then we're good to go.'

'Huh?' said Joe.

'Violetta, you pretend to be Theodore Flunk,' instructed Jim. 'And you, Joe. You repeat everything you hear coming through your earpiece.'

'Erm . . . OK,' Joe said, feeling a nervous sweat gather on his brow.

'I'll be upstairs,' said Jim, dashing out of the room. 'On my say so, guys. GO!'

'So then Joe, how do you expect to continue as Prime Minister when you walk so silly?' Violetta began with the first thing that popped into her head.

'Joe, can you hear me?' Jim's voice came through Joe's earpiece.

'YES!' Joe yelled out.

'Yes? That's your answer?' Violetta asked.

Joe concentrated on the noise in his ear. He cleared his throat and smiled.

'That's right,' he said. 'I do expect to continue as Prime Minister and I would respectfully ask Mr Flunk to stick to relevant questions, rather than personal attacks.' He paused. 'No one likes a bully, after all.'

Violetta looked impressed. 'Slick,' she said. 'Very slick.'

Joe beamed.

'That went well. OK, I might feel better if you could be in my earpiece Jim, in case I freeze, you know?'

'Sure—anything you say, boss,' Jim grinned.

'Good boy.' Violetta patted Joe on the head and ruffled his hair.

'You know,' said Joe, happily, 'if you think the blue suit is best, I'll go with that.'

WE'LL LET YOU KNOW

'Good morning,' Ajay said into the intercom. 'My name is Ajay Patel. I'm here to see Theodore Flunk?'

There was a two-second pause before the door buzzed and Ajay took a deep breath and walked into Flunk HQ. He wasn't sure what he was expecting, but it all seemed a little bit grubby—Ajay had never seen so many horrible shades of brown in one place. People were running around with pieces of paper, looking as though they had a lot to do and not enough time to do it. Not that surprising since it was the day of the big debate. Everyone was working at full capacity.

'He'll be with you in a second,' a receptionist said, taking Ajay's hoodie and hanging it up. 'Do take a seat.' She pointed to a faded, old, chocolate-brown sofa.

Ajay sat down on the sofa and looked around. The offices were divided into little glass boxes, and in each one somebody sat at a computer, or was on a phone, swigging coffee and looking strung out. Ajay stared ahead to the largest glass box, where blinds hung down from the ceiling. Despite this, Ajay could clearly see through the slats. Theodore was in there— he'd know that spindly body anywhere. He was standing up, jabbing his finger in the air and saying something in an angry voice, which was getting angrier and louder by the second.

'OH, JUST SHOVE IT, JOHNSON!' yelled Flunk, finally.

'Mr Flunk is ready for you now,' the receptionist told Ajay.

Ajay gulped, and as he walked anxiously towards Flunk's door, a man came out.

'Great meeting, boss!' the man said, turning and smiling at Theodore, despite the fact that Theodore was scowling back at him. This must be Johnson, Ajay thought. He looked very cheery considering he'd just been verbally abused. Ajay was beginning to regret this meeting. He didn't fancy being shouted at.

'Ajay!' Theodore was beaming at him. It was a slightly evil smile, but it was still a smile and Ajay relaxed.

'Is now a good time?' he asked.

'Oh yes!' said Flunk. 'Don't worry about all the shouting. We all shout at each other here. It's harmless bants, Ajay. And everyone's a bit worked up, what with the imminent election! I'm so glad you've come to join us. It must be nice to come and work somewhere you'll be appreciated.'

'Yeah, about that—' Ajay started.

'We're so looking forward to having you on board!' Flunk continued. 'I've invented a whole new role for you. Your job title will be "Background Investigator and Project Manager". Cool, huh? Makes you sound like a cop or something.' Theodore grinned.

'Investigator? Project Manager?' Ajay frowned. 'I thought you wanted me to come on board and help with strategy.'

'Oh no. We have a million people who can do that. Your job is special. You're in charge of digging up the dirt on Joe Perkins.' Flunk rubbed his hands together with glee. 'He stabbed you in the back, Ajay. Now it's time for revenge!'

'So, you didn't want me for my highly tuned

strategic brain?' Ajay asked.

'No, my dear boy, I need all of Joe's dirty secrets so that we can destroy him. What lies behind the squeaky-clean image? The butter-wouldn't-melt façade? Sure, that awful speech ditching the Green Space initiative made a dent in his reputation but annoyingly the public seem to be giving him the benefit of the doubt. I want to know if Perkins has ever lied to his mum, or kicked a puppy, or stolen a lollipop. Does he drink orange juice straight from the carton? Does he share his Easter eggs or hog them to himself? Maybe he likes to dress up as Batman at the weekend? I want info on every silly and embarrassing thing he's ever done before tonight's debate. I want to reveal the real Joe Perkins to the country!'

Ajay crossed his arms over his T-shirt and stared at him.

'What's the matter, boy?' Flunk's excitement was fading.

'You know,' said Ajay, 'for a while there I really thought you needed my help for something important, something where my unique skill set would be put to good use. But it's obvious you're just a BIG, FAT MEANIE!'

'I beg your pardon?' Flunk said in shock. 'Are you turning me down?'

'Yes. I was going to anyway. That's what I came here to tell you. I thought it was the courteous thing to do since you had offered me a proper job. I was gonna text, but I thought you deserved better.'

'Oh, you kids with your principles and morals!' said Flunk in disgust. 'That's not how you win elections, you little fool. You win elections with ruthless and sneaky behaviour. By manipulating and twisting the truth. By humiliating your opponent!'

Ajay shrugged. 'Good luck with that, Mr Flunk, but I don't want any part of it.'

'Good riddance then, you ungrateful brat!' Flunk roared, slamming his office door in Ajay's face.

Johnson was walking back to his glass box at Flunk HQ when he heard a mobile phone ringing from somewhere. Looking left and right, he frowned, trying to work out where it was coming from. And then his gaze fell on a hoodie hanging up on the hat stand in reception. It belonged to Ajay Patel. Johnson hesitated for a split second before curiosity got the better of him.

'Hello, Ajay Patel's phone,' he said. 'No, he's in a meeting with Theodore Flunk. Yes, that is what I said. Can I take a message—?'

But whoever it was had hung up, and now Ajay was storming down the corridor with a face like thunder and Johnson was still holding his phone.

'Oh. Your phone . . . it was . . .'

But Ajay just whipped the phone out of his hand and grabbed his hoodie.

'I'm going!' he said. 'Your boss is an absolute monster!'

'Ooh, I know,' Johnson said proudly.

Ajay shook his head at him, sadly. 'I really hope Flunk loses this election to Joe Perkins,' he said. 'And common decency will win out.'

'Common decency?' Johnson looked bewildered.

'What does that even mean?'

Ajay rolled his eyes. 'See ya, wouldn't wanna be ya!'

'JOOOOOHNSON!' Flunk's muffled roar could be heard from his glass box. 'THROW HIM OUT!'

'Is everything OK?' Jim looked at Joe, who was standing looking forlorn with his phone in his hand.

'What? Oh fine . . .' Joe said, vaguely, putting away his mobile.

'Good,' Jim said, looking at his watch, 'because it's time.'

'Time?'

'Time for the debate, Joe—and with me in your ear, you have nothing to worry about!' Jim said.

Suddenly, outside the bus there was the sound of a distant whirring, like a helicopter.

'Come on,' said Jim. 'Let's do this!'

As Joe got off the bus, the wind whipped around him. Quickly, the sunshine disappeared and the temperature dropped. It felt like a total eclipse of the sun. Joe put his hands over his eyes to protect them from the dust being kicked up by whatever was up there causing a mini-hurricane.

'What on earth—?' he murmured, as Jim and Violetta walked off the bus to join him.

The sound was almost deafening now as a spotlight appeared, beaming down and blinding them for a second.

'Hello, down there,' came a voice through what sounded like a loudhailer. 'Take me to your leader . . .'

'Ooh. That's me,' said Joe, waving. 'Yoo-hoo! I'm here! It's me, Joe Perkins.'

'Prime Minister, it's Charlie James here, welcoming you to the heli-telly-studio!'

'Erm . . . how do we get up there?' Joe said, squinting up as the dust and leaves swirled round and round.

A rope ladder appeared, dangling in front of them.

'I suppose it could be fun,' Joe smiled, seizing the bottom rung. 'To infinity and beyooooooond!'

UP IN THE SKY

'Whoaaa! That was amazing,' Joe said, stepping into Channel 10's heli-telly-studio. He looked over his shoulder to see Violetta and Jim arriving through the portal, too, looking like a couple of kids getting off a fairground ride that had gone too fast.

'OMG!' Joe walked around the giant studio and whistled. 'I wish all TV studios were like this.'

'Yeah, that's what I thought at first.' Charlie's voice came from somewhere to Joe's side. 'But I'm begging you. Please rescue me. Take me with you, back to the land dwellers . . .'

Joe turned and came face to face with a man who

had fluorescent green skin.

'Charlie James,' said the man. 'Excuse my appearance.'

'Wow, your face,' said Joe. 'What would you even call that shade of green?'

'Vivid Pea?' Jim offered.

'Please don't mention food,' Charlie said. 'I've been stuck up here for nearly two weeks. I'm so sick. Please, just put me out of my misery. Hit me over the head with a chair. End it all now. Have you any idea how much make-up I have on, just so I look human? It takes hours. They coat me like they're frosting a cupcake . . . oh, I shouldn't have said "cupcake". Oh, oh dear . . .' Charlie ran off to find a loo.

'Why don't I take you to your dressing room?' a helpful assistant said, ushering them past the cameras. 'We're just putting the finishing touches to the studio before the broadcast. They're predicting record viewing figures for the TV debate,' she added. 'It's all so exciting!'

'Is Charlie OK?' Joe asked, concerned.

'He'll be fine,' she said. 'We're not expecting any

turbulence.'

'Really?' Theodore Flunk appeared out of a tiny dressing room. 'I wouldn't be so sure about that.'

'Flunk,' Joe said, narrowing his eyes.

'Perkins.' Flunk flashed him a smug grin. 'I look forward to wiping the floor with you later. I hope you've prepared for this debate. I don't plan on taking any prisoners tonight.'

'Oh, we're definitely prepared.' Joe glanced at Jim and Violetta. If only Theodore knew what he had up his sleeve. Joe smiled, though couldn't ignore the nervous feeling in his tummy. He was doing the right thing, wasn't he?

'Yes, well, I'm prepared, too,' Theodore said childishly. 'Very, very prepared.'

'Really, is that why your flies are undone?' said Joe.

'What?!'

'Ha! Made you look.' Joe laughed.

'I hate you, Joe,' snarled Flunk. 'You're finished. I will find a way to finish this so that you're properly finished!'

'You keep saying "finish" and "finished", Sir,' Johnson chipped in, unhelpfully.

'SHUT UP!' Theodore snapped, grabbing Johnson and pushing him back inside his dressing room.

'Classic,' Joe said, looking around for Ajay without thinking.

'I don't think making childish jokes at the expense of the opposition will help us,' Violetta said. 'He's out to get you now.'

'He can try,' said Joe. 'But with you guys on my side, nothing can go wrong.' Joe popped his earpiece in and tapped his ear. 'Testing one, two, three . . .'

Violetta spoke into a discreet phone. 'Hello, can you hear me?'

'Yes, you're coming through loud and clear,' said Joe.

'Now, it can get pretty confusing listening and speaking simultaneously. So, only one person can talk at a time to keep things simple. OK? We wouldn't want anything to go wrong, now, would we?'

'Got it! Now I'm off to the loo before the debate starts,' said Joe. 'Back in a mo.'

'Thanks for letting us know,' Violetta smiled tightly.

Violetta pressed her hands together with excitement when Joe was out of earshot. 'This is going to be so perfect!' she said. 'We can say whatever we like into my phone and to his earpiece and Joe will say it. He's so unsure of himself these days he doesn't trust himself with any decisions anymore, it's brilliant. Joe is doomed!'

Jim nodded. 'But we don't want any of this coming back on us. For Joe's downfall to be flawless, it needs to look as though he's destroyed himself.'

'How can we be sure that once we've got rid of Joe, Flunk won't still win?' Violetta asked Jim.

'Ha! I have a hundred fake stories about Flunk,' Jim laughed. 'He's easy pickings.'

Listening outside Joe's dressing room, Johnson couldn't believe what he'd just overheard. This was mind-blowing information and he needed to tell Flunk.

'Five minutes everyone!' Charlie said, looking slightly less green. He clapped his hands. 'Right, anyone who isn't Joe Perkins or Theodore Flunk, please stand at the side and you can watch in the wings. Flunk, Perkins, when the lights come on, walk slowly to the podium. Be careful, it's a bit wobbly, being up in the sky and all that . . .' Charlie clutched his stomach. 'Oh dear, let's get started.'

'I hope you've been practising your walk,' Theodore whispered unpleasantly to Joe.

'Actually, I have.' Joe looked over at Jim and Violetta and gave them the thumbs up, then tapped his ear discreetly.

Jim and Violetta were ready. They were just about to retire to the dressing room to start feeding Joe lines, when the producer stopped them. 'Phones in here please,' she said holding out a basket. 'And the dressing rooms are out of bounds once the debate starts so you'll have to stay here I'm afraid.'

'What?' Violetta and Jim went pale.

'We get a lot of static this high up. A mobile phone can cause a buzzing sound on TV. Please, put it in the box until the recording is over.'

Violetta reluctantly put her phone in the basket.

'Once we go live and the lights go down, I'll steal the phone back. No one will notice, they'll be too busy with the show,' Violetta whispered to Jim.

'WELCOME TO THE BIG ELECTION DEBATE, LIVE FROM THE SKY!' Charlie said, as the cameras rolled. 'I'd like to welcome our leadership candidates: current Prime Minister, Joe Perkins, who's hoping to be returned to office, and Theodore Flunk, the man who wants the top job.' Charlie smiled, his heavy make-up hiding the green hue that had returned to his skin. 'LET THE DEBATE BEGIN!'

'Now!' hissed Jim, as the lights lowered and the music started. 'Everyone's distracted.'

Violetta didn't need telling twice. She nipped stealthily over to the producer's basket of devices and rescued her phone, subtly switching it on then putting it in her pocket. As Jim gave her a furtive thumbs up, she made her way to where he was sitting in a quiet corner of the studio.

'First question is for Mr Flunk,' began Charlie. 'What will be your top priority as Prime Minister?'

'Well, to undo everything that Perkins has ever done!' Theodore said arrogantly. 'He has been the worst Prime Minister since the last worst one. He has made this country into a laughing stock, I mean out-lawing the handshake and replacing it with the fist bump? I ask you!'

'And what about you, Mr Perkins?' Charlie said.

'My first job will to be to get back to business!' Violetta whispered into the phone.

'Mr Perkins?' Charlie asked.

Joe tapped his ear. He couldn't hear a thing.

'PRIME MINISTER?' Charlie tried again.

Meanwhile, Violetta looked down at her phone and noticed it wasn't actually her phone at all.

'OMG,' she mouthed at Jim. 'OMG.'

'We're waiting for your answer, Mr Perkins.'

Charlie's tone was steely.

'Um,' Joe swallowed. 'Um. Well. I mean . . . the very first thing I'll do is . . .'

'Yes?' prompted Charlie.

Just in time, Joe heard a voice through his ear-piece.

'My first job is to do a BIG DANCE! With my PANTS ON MY HEAD,' he said, pasting a smile on his face.

'What?' Charlie asked.

'Joe is being fed lines from someone else,' Violetta whispered angrily. 'Someone's on to us, Jim.'

SPACE ODDITY

'Could you say that again?' Charlie cupped his hand to his ear. 'I think I misheard.'

'Um. Don't want to?' Joe said, blushing furiously.

'Hey!' The producer strode over to Johnson, whose face was pressed up to a phone. 'I've told you once! No phones!'

'GET OFF MY PHONE!' Johnson yelled, as the producer made a grab for it.

'Actually, it's my phone.' Violetta was on her feet, indignant. 'You're a thief, Johnson!'

'Well, you've stolen mine,' Johnson snapped at

her. 'So *you're* a thief!'

'For goodness' sake!' the producer said, shaking her head in disbelief.

'Give it back!' Violetta cried.

'NO!' Johnson yelled out.

The producer grabbed Johnson's phone in one, swift move. 'YOU'RE BOTH IDIOTS!'

As Violetta lunged to get hers back, she smacked it like a volleyball out of the producer's hand and high up in the air, where it boomeranged off a piece of equipment and then disappeared somewhere in the darkness.

Back in the debate, Charlie James was looking concerned.

'Are you feeling OK, Prime Minister?'

'Not really, no,' Joe said, undoing his tie, then wincing at the sound of something loud in his ear.

Violetta nudged Jim. 'Joe's still getting something through his earpiece. The phone must be feeding him sounds still. We just need to hope he gives us a clue,' she said, catching Joe's eye.

'We've lost the phone,' she mouthed at him, 'and we need to find it.'

For a moment, Joe looked blank, but then he nodded, and soon his eyes lit up, and a smile appeared on his face as he started talking. 'Man, I'm bursting for the loo.'

'Prime Minister?' Charlie looked horrified.

Joe blew a huge raspberry in response. 'Pooh! Shouldn't have had all those beans for lunch. They always make me fart like a trooper.' Joe looked meaningfully at Violetta and Jim.

Charlie shut his eyes. 'Please don't talk about food and flatulence,' he said. 'I was just starting to feel normal.'

'The toilet,' Jim hissed. 'The phone's in the toilet!'

Leaving Joe to continue making a complete spectacle of himself, Violetta crept off, charging into the toilet, and immediately spotted her phone which had landed on a trolley next to the door. Just as she was picking it up, a technician came out of the cubicle and washed his hands.

'I'd leave it about ten minutes,' he said, apologetically.

Holding her nose, Violetta returned to the studio, where Charlie had called an ad break and was checking his notes. Theodore was talking in an angry whisper to Johnson, while Joe was jumping up and down trying to get Violetta's attention.

'Get me out of this mess!' Joe mouthed. 'I need to start making sense or we're going to lose.'

Violetta tapped her nose at him conspiratorially. 'Leave it with me,' she mouthed back.

'Welcome back,' Charlie said, taking a swig of water. 'Now let's see if our current Prime Minister can get back on track after a frankly alarming first answer!'

'It's OK, Joe,' Violetta whispered into her phone, and through his earpiece. 'You're in safe hands now. Let's talk about something positive. What about that great idea you had about moving to the moon?

Joe smiled uneasily. *I mean, Jim said the idea was genius and he does know best, right?!*

'OK,' said Charlie. 'Let's talk about your big

ideas, Prime Minister.'

'I THINK WE SHOULD ALL MOVE TO THE MOON!' Joe cried. 'IT'S A NEW START FOR . . . EVERYONE!'

Joe looked to Jim who was giving him the big thumbs up. Joe took a deep breath and pulled out his earpiece. 'YES, WE NEED A FRESH START, SO LET'S ALL MOVE TO THE MOON! Vote for me and you could be on a one-way flight to outer space!'

'Oh, Joe . . .' Violetta sat back, smirking.

'Perfect,' Jim smiled. 'He's toast.'

'Just a minute . . .' Charlie stepped closer to Joe, pointing at the earpiece. 'What's that in your hand, Mr Perkins?'

'You idiot, put it back in your ear!' Violetta screeched, but it was too late. Charlie had already grabbed it out of Joe's hand and was holding it up to his own.

'Is that Violetta?' he said. 'Is this the Prime Minister's director of strategy feeding him lines?' Charlie looked coldly at Joe. 'You were trying to *cheat* your way to victory?'

For a second Joe looked horrified. And then suddenly his shoulders slumped in defeat. Joe looked directly at the camera, exhausted. 'Yes,' he said quietly.

'SHUT UP, YOU MORON!' Violetta roared, before realizing she was live on television. 'Wasn't anyone listening when he said he wanted to MOVE TO THE MOON?! He was only meant to destroy himself, not me!' Violetta pointed at Jim. 'The Rottweiler is behind this!'

'ER, EXCUSE ME? YOU CAME TO ME!' Jim yelled, outraged. 'IT WAS YOUR IDEA TO BRING DOWN JOE PERKINS SO THAT YOU COULD HAVE HIS JOB—AFTER YOU'D RUINED FLUNK'S CHANCES WITH ALL THOSE FAKE STORIES I WAS GOING TO MAKE UP . . .' Jim stopped and bit his lip. 'Oops.'

'Good grief.' Charlie was shocked. 'What a fiasco. The General Election is days away.' He pointed at Theodore Flunk. 'And we're facing up to the fact that this piece of work is the only HONEST candidate.'

'I know!' Theodore grinned, clapping his hands together in delight.

I DON'T THINK YOU'RE READY FOR THIS JELLY

'Young man, come on out of there!'

'No.'

'I'm your mother. You have to obey me, it's the law!' Joe's mum said.

'I want to be on my own,' Joe said.

'Joe? Are you eating what I think you are?'

'No,' Joe said, lying.

'Right, I'm breaking the door down.' She took a step back, pacing out her run-up, but just as she was about to charge, Joe opened the door. He was standing in his pants, eating from a bowl of jelly with the TV remote in his hand.

'Give me that,' she said, taking the bowl of jelly off Joe. 'How much have you had?'

'This is my fifteenth bowl.' Joe looked sad.

'I'll put the kettle on.' She sighed. 'What is it with you and eating jelly in your pants?'

'I like pants and I like jelly,' Joe said. 'What more do you need to know? Now leave me be. There's a new flavour—lime and blackcurrant cocktail—I want to try.'

'You're mixing jellies? Oh, I can't have that. Consider this an intervention!'

When Joe had first become the Prime Minister, he and Ajay decided they wanted an entire room dedicated to all kinds of jelly. In recent times, it had become a bolthole for Joe whenever he was feeling blue. Unlike politics and people, jelly had never let him down. Neither had underpants, to be honest. Although if Joe didn't stop eating jelly he'd need a bigger pair.

His mum gazed around at the empty bowls everywhere and spoons littering the carpet. 'Joe, you need to pull yourself together. What are you going to do?'

After the horrendous big debate the day before, Joe had driven straight back to Downing Street and shut himself inside the jelly room. Violetta and Jim had scarpered and now he was all alone.

'Do about what? The election is lost, I'll have to move out in a couple of days so that Theodore can move in. And fair's fair, he may be a nasty man, but at least he didn't try and cheat his way to power. Jenkins was right, elections can turn people strange. Look at me! I'm a disgrace. I let myself believe that winning was all that mattered, even though it meant hurting everyone around me and making some really, really, really bad decisions.'

'You were fine until that Violetta Crump and Jim Jones turned you inside out,' said his mum. 'Don't despair. While there's time, there's always a chance to put things right, Joe.'

'No, it's too late. No one wants to be my friend,

let alone vote for me.'

'Well *someone's* keen to talk to you.' She looked down at the notifications on Joe's phone. 'You have thirteen missed calls from Alice.'

'I've let her down the most,' Joe sighed, looking ashamed.

'Well, feeling sorry for yourself isn't helping anyone.'

'Oh Mum, leave me alone, all I want to do is watch TV,' Joe said, grabbing back the remote. 'I want to watch CBeebies.'

'You need to snap out of it, Joe. You're still the Prime Minister, and frankly this is undignified,' she said, looking him up and down.

'Well, don't worry, I won't be Prime Minister for long,' Joe said, pressing the remote again. 'Then you won't have to worry about me embarrassing you anymore. I can sit around in my pants all day then.'

'No, you can't. There is no job in the world that lets you sit around all day like this. Not Prime Minister, or school boy. And yes, you may not have long left in this house, but that doesn't give you the right to give up. People need you.'

'Oh yeah, like who?' Joe asked miserably.

'Well, like her,' Mum said, pointing at the TV.

Joe peered forward and there was Alice on the TV. She was standing in the rain, holding up a sign saying, "Save Our Parks". Joe turned up the volume so he could hear the news report.

A reporter was interviewing Alice. 'She once had the ear of the Prime Minister, but now Alice is all on her own again, fighting for something she really believes in. We spoke to her earlier today.'

'Yeah, I know it's just me out here on my own, and maybe Joe Perkins changed his mind about helping me, but that isn't to say that I should just give up. Every child deserves to have a park to play in and I know that I have to do what I can to make it happen. So far, I've organized a petition and it's got twenty names!' she grinned. 'Oh wait, my Nan's signed it twice. Nearly twenty . . .'

'What an inspiration! While politicians fight and threaten to move us all to the moon, at least one girl is keeping her feet on the ground,' the reporter said. 'Back to you in the heli-studio . . .'

Joe hit the mute button on the TV. 'She's still out there protesting,' Joe said, with admiration.

'Do you know what would really help her now?' Mum said in a gentle, kind voice.

'What?' Joe replied.

'If you ate some more jelly in your pants!' she

snapped. 'Oh no, wait, that wouldn't help her at all.'

'Where's my socks? I need to go and see Alice!' Joe said, standing up and clicking his fingers.

'At last, he's back!' Mum said, clapping her hands.

'Stop here,' Joe said to the driver.

'Sure thing, boss,' the driver replied.

Joe had arrived outside Alice's house. He hopped out of the car and made a dash to the front door, giving it a hard thump. The rain was pouring down and Joe manoeuvred himself as best he could, to shelter from the worst of it.

'Hello?' a muffled voice came through the door.

'Hello?' Joe answered back. He peered down to look through the letter box, and gave a jump.

'Wha!' someone screamed.

'Sorry, I didn't realize you were . . . so close. I'm here to see Alice,' Joe said.

There was a creak as the door opened, to reveal a grumpy-looking old man.

'What do you want to see Alice about? Are you a boyfriend?'

'No! No, I just want to help her with her campaign to make more green space.'

'All right, one second . . .' The man, who must have been Alice's dad, yelled up the stairs, 'Alice, there's a lad from school here. He wants to talk to you.'

'Well, actually I'm not from . . . never mind,' Joe said, not wanting to go into it.

'Dad!' Alice said, appearing at the top of the stairs. 'This is the Prime Minister!'

'Prime Minister? This lad? No way, oh my goodness me, I knew I knew you from somewhere, but I thought you were the paperboy or something.'

'Well, give it a week and I might be,' Joe smiled.

'Dad,' Alice said, 'could you get us some squash and biscuits?'

'I'll get the posh stuff!' Alice's dad said, snapping

his fingers and scuttling off to the kitchen.

'There's really no need . . .' Joe said, waving after him, but it was too late, he'd already gone.

Alice led Joe into the living room where they sat in uncomfortable silence. 'I just wanted to say . . .'

'Sorry?' Alice interrupted.

'Sorry,' Joe said. 'I saw you on the news. I've messed up badly and I think I'm going to lose this election and then the Green Space initiative will never get off the ground.' Joe hung his head, miserably.

'Win or lose, it doesn't mean I'm going to stop trying,' Alice said.

'Winning is all I've been thinking about,' Joe sighed.

'Well, that's silly,' Alice said.

'Is it?' Joe asked.

'Listen, when I was running for school council, I knew I could never beat Joanne Green.'

'Who's Joanne Green?'

'She's the most popular girl in school. Her hair is perfect and she has a pony. Anyway, everyone loved her. I knew that if I tried to be like her it wouldn't work, because well, my hair has a mind of its own and I'm allergic to ponies.'

'Oh,' Joe said.

'Then I thought, I could be the opposite of Joanne Green, and be everything she isn't.'

'That's a good idea,' Joe said.

'No, it isn't.' Alice corrected him. 'That would never have worked. What if she said or did something I agreed with, then I'd have to do the opposite, even if that meant doing the wrong thing?'

'Right, I follow,' Joe said. 'But I know you did win in the end, so what was your secret?'

'There is no secret, that's the point. You work hard and be the best version of yourself you can be. If people don't want to vote for you, then that's their choice, but being true to yourself is the best chance you have of winning. So that's what I did. I told people what I thought, and I told people what I would do if I was school councillor,' Alice shrugged.

'And you won.'

'I did! People liked what I had to say, and the fact

that Joanne Green had to compete in a gymkhana that day also swung it for me. You see, Joe, if you pretend to be something you're not, and people vote for you, then you have to keep pretending you're that person forever.'

'Why didn't I know this?' Joe said, slumping into his seat again.

'Because sometimes you only know what the right thing was with hindsight. But you're lucky.'

'Lucky, how?' Joe asked.

'Lucky because the moment hasn't gone. You haven't lost yet,' Alice said.

'The election is in two days' time and the last anyone heard from me I was telling them to move to the moon! I'm so low down in the polls you need a telescope to see how far out of the race I am,' Joe said.

'Who's for squash?' Alice's dad said, coming into the room and wheeling a trolley with the finest china on. 'I'll pour.' Alice's dad lifted an ornamental teapot and poured out some orange squash.

'Hobnob, your highness?' he said, offering one

to Joe on a decorative saucer.

'Er, thank you,' Joe replied, sipping from the tiny teacup. 'There's no way I can win though, Alice.'

'Haven't you listened to a word I've said?! Winning doesn't matter!' Alice sighed. 'It's about being yourself. Don't think about winning, just . . .'

'Try my best to put things right and speak from the heart?'

'Now you're getting it,' Alice smiled.

'OK,' Joe said, standing up and finishing the rest of his drink. 'Will you help me? I need all the help I can get. Plus, if I start going on about how we should all live underwater or grow an extra head, you can snap me out of it.'

'Of course!' Alice smiled.

'Yeah, Alice—go get 'em!' her dad squealed.

'Where to first?' Alice asked excitedly.

'Hmm, I fancy a bit of shopping . . .' Joe smiled.

WE GET BY WITH A LITTLE HELP FROM OUR FRIENDS

The bell jangled as Joe opened the door to a tiny shop which was full of old furniture which smelled of the past, but in a good way, like old furniture should smell.

'I'll be with you in a second, I'm a bit rushed off my feet,' a familiar voice shouted from the back of the shop. 'You're my second customer of the day. Well, second customer ever, in fact. Is there anything particular you're after?'

'Some help from an old friend—and maybe a

bow tie or two.'

'Prime Minister!! And Alice too!!' Jenkins' head shot out from behind a curtain. 'How are you, Sir?'

'Not so good, Jenkins,' Joe said, his lip wobbling a bit, like he might cry. Were you allowed to cry as a Prime Minister? Or would that lose you 1.2648583537% votes, he wondered.

'Well, bow ties I have plenty of. I suppose advice can be forthcoming too, but I think I should put the kettle on for that. And if it's a friend you're looking for too, I think I have something round the back that might suit, if you'd like to take a look?'

Joe scratched his head and followed Jenkins round to the back of the shop, where Ajay was lounging in his underpants on an antique chair, engrossed in his PlayStation, a bowl with the remains of jelly in it by his feet. 'Ajay?!' Joe cried. 'How long have you been here?'

'A while,' said Ajay, shyly.

'I've told him repeatedly to put on his trousers and go easy on the jelly,' said Jenkins. 'But would he listen?'

'I see he's wearing a bow tie. That's something at least,' said Joe. 'But you should really do what Jenkins says, there's a girl present.'

'Cripes,' Alice gasped. 'Aren't you a bit old for Thomas the Tank Engine pants?'

'They're so comfy though. Oh Joe, it's been so awful,' Ajay sobbed. 'What have we done? Violetta and Jim played us off against each other and we totally fell for it!'

'I know!' Joe said. 'Listen, I would hug you, but you're only in your pants. Do you feel ready for trousers?'

'YES, YES I DO!' Ajay sobbed, slipping on his slacks.

'I thought you were working for Flunk?' Joe said.

'Yeah, Flunk offered me a job, but I told him to stick it,' said Ajay proudly. 'He's a bad person, and now he's going to live in *our* house. He's going to be Prime Minister. Oh yikes! I think I went for the trousers too soon—where's my jelly?!'

'No, Ajay, you can do it!'

'I'm sorry about the Green Space initiative,' said Ajay. 'They told me you'd changed your mind and wanted to turn it into a big office block. I guess they told *you* it was all *my* idea and that I wanted to quit.'

'They played us like a couple of cheap fiddles at a barn dance, Ajay,' Joe sighed.

'Yes, yes!' Alice snapped. 'You let me down, you're sorry, blah, blah, but the real question is, what are you going to do about it?'

'You're right,' Joe said. 'We need make stuff happen.'

'Joe needs you, too, Jenkins,' Alice said before turning to Joe and Ajay and looking at them seriously. 'If we really do believe in the Green Space initiative, and we still want to make the world a better place, then we cannot just spend the rest of our lives eating jelly in our undercrackers.'

'Wise words, and a heck of a campaign slogan if you don't mind me saying,' Jenkins said. 'But I have to say that it isn't looking good. I've been through many political battles, but never one where we're at such a disadvantage.'

'What about a multimedia Instagram story . . .' Ajay started.

'No, Ajay,' Joe snapped. 'No more gimmicks. I just need to tell the truth and let the people decide.' Joe smiled. 'I don't know if it'll work, but it's all I have left. No more lions, no more rapping, just me being myself. I just hope it's not too late. Ajay, Jenkins, how quickly can we get a live TV broadcast set up so that I can speak to the nation?'

'As soon as we get back to No.10, Sir,' Jenkins said.

'Great, so we're good to go.'

'But we need time to write a speech, and so you

can rehearse and prepare,' Jenkins said, looking at his watch.

'Oh, I know exactly what I'm going to say,' Joe smiled. 'I'm going to say sorry.'

Later that day, Joe stood in front of a camera and gave his speech to the nation.

'Good evening people of Britain. It's a privilege to be able to talk to you as your Prime Minister. Whether I shall remain your Prime Minister is up to you. You'll cast your vote in a couple of days and decide who gets to lead this great country.

'I have spent this campaign going around the country, getting into the most ridiculous scrapes and making the headlines in all the newspapers, but there's something I have neglected to do—the most important thing any politician or Prime Minister can ever do, and that's listen. I've become so consumed by the idea of winning, that I became someone else. Someone I didn't like. The more I wanted to win, the more I lost sight of what was really important. I made terrible decisions and I let people down.

'I became lost and out of touch. Like, for instance, well, you know, wanting to move to the moon. As mistakes go, that was a humdinger. The idea is ridiculous! Literally, what was I thinking?! I am so sorry—I have been the nincompoop-iest of nincompoops.

'Over the last couple of weeks, I nearly lost my best friend, my family, and the staff who are my second family. It's to them that I also now say sorry. If you decide in two days' time that I'm not the right person to lead the country, I will quite understand. I don't know if I deserve a second chance to be honest, but I hope over the next couple of days I can show you what I really want to do, if I am lucky enough to stick around.

'I'm going to be walking around and meeting people. No more campaign buses and no more parachutes, just me talking about what I want for the country and, most importantly, listening to what you the people want. My first priority is going to be building a park on every street corner, where kids can play, and grow flowers and vegetables. I lied about wanting to cancel my Green Space initiative because I thought that was what you wanted to hear. But I have learnt that doing the right thing—the thing you most believe in, in your heart of hearts—is more important than being popular. I want to make the world a better place, otherwise what's the point of being in politics?

'Thank you for listening to me this evening. I believe in this wonderful, occasionally drizzly, land and its wonderful people. Good night and thank you.'

'And, we're clear!' Ajay said, operating the camera.

'Perfect!' Jenkins said.

'Good on you, Joe,' said Alice.

'Well, thank you for making me see sense,' Joe said. 'High fives?'

'Oh my. I'm so sorry I ever doubted you,' Ajay turned to Joe. 'This feels like more than a high-five moment. Can I have a hug? I love you, big guy. Come to Ajay!'

'Arrrgh! OK Ajay,' Joe wriggled in his friend's arms. 'COME ON JENKINS AND ALICE, GET IN

HERE! I LOVE YOU GUYS!!' Ajay cried, pulling his happy/crying human emoji face.

'Alice, help me!' Joe said.

'Nah, I want to join in too!' she said, jumping in.

'AAAARGH, YOU'RE SQUISHING THE PRIME MINISTER! THAT HAS TO BE AGAINST THE LAW!' Joe laughed.

THE BOYS ARE
BACK IN TOWN

O ver the last two days of the campaign, Joe went out and met as many people as he could. Some people wanted to hear him out and he did his best to explain. Some people just threw rotten fruit at him and Joe tried to take it with good grace. Some of it was actually still tasty.

Occasionally, it felt as though things had changed, not just for Joe, but for the whole country. People started to come together to listen to one another, even when they might disagree.

Joe met people from all walks of life: young, old,

rich, and poor. He told people what he planned if he stayed in the job and he listened to how they thought he could be a better Prime Minister. *You liked the Green Space initiative? Well, I'm bringing it back! You want to build your own house on the moon? I'm afraid that's a big no from me, sorry. And that goes for feeding lions, too.*

There were no TV crews, no make-up assistants, no social-media hashtags, and no team of speech-writers. Just Joe, Ajay, Jenkins, and Alice. By the morning of the General Election, Joe felt tired but more revived than ever. He knew that if he was going to lose, he was glad he had at least been honest. He knew he had made mistakes—we all do—it's how you pick yourself up afterwards that's important.

At the very last public meeting of the campaign, Joe stood before the crowd of people. 'TV news is a twenty-four-hour-a-day business. But despite us having more news channels than we know what to do with, there is no time to actually *say* anything. And then, just as the election builds to fever-pitch, it all stops and it's just down to you: the voters. The future is in your hands.'

The crowd had roared with approval and only two people had thrown a rotten cabbage.

As for Violetta and Jim? There would be no more comebacks for either of them. Of course, they planted some ridiculous stories about Joe in the papers, but it just wasn't the same, now that the public had seen Violetta and Jim's true colours during the live debate. No one was taking their calls. Jim's bus and high-tech data system were history. The last Joe heard, Violetta was thinking of setting up her own political party, or that both Violetta and Jim were planning on leaving the country and never coming back, perhaps hoping to find an island where they could rule their own little bit of land.

'Strange day, Jenkins, election day. What do you think our chances are?' Joe said, sitting up in bed.

'I can say this with complete certainty—I have absolutely no idea, Sir.' Jenkins pulled out his ceremonial sword to lop off the top of Joe's morning egg.

'I thought I would go out and meet some more voters today and then maybe see if anyone fancies a kick about in the park before we watch the results.'

'Sounds like a plan, Sir.'

After meeting more people that day, and clarifying some more of his election points ('No, you have it the wrong way round: I say yes to the Green Space initiative and definitely a no bungalows on Jupiter'), Joe enjoyed a spot of attackers verses defenders down the park, before heading back to No. 10 Downing Street. Everyone was there: Joe and Ajay's mums, Jenkins, and Alice and her dad, too.

'Wow, what a place!' Alice's dad mused. 'This is posher than the place I hired out for my 50th birthday party. Who knew politics was so exciting!'

They all settled down to watch the results. Later, they would either have the party of their lives or a funeral for Joe's time as Prime Minister. Either way, Joe felt OK. He would never stop arguing for the things he believed in, and knowing that was a good feeling. He'd forgotten how much he liked himself when he was just being honest.

BONG!

Joe snapped out of his daydream to the sound of Big Ben chiming ten o'clock.

'Sir, the polls have closed and the results are coming in—good luck!'

Ajay switched on Channel 10 news.

'Hello, here I am, back on terra firma again!' Charlie Jones said, getting out of the heli-telly-studio and kissing the floor. 'I'm alive, ALIVE! Now, to the person who invented this thing, fire them and burn it.'

'It's time for the results! As Big Ben strikes ten and the polls close, we make our first predictions.'

Joe grabbed his mum's hand and Ajay grabbed Jenkins' hand.

'We predict,' said Charlie, 'that Theodore Flunk will be the next Prime Minister of Great Britain. Joe Perkins has lost . . .'

There was silence. Joe turned to look around the room. Alice had tears in her eyes, as did Jenkins. Ajay's mouth was open, as though frozen in time. For once, no one had anything to say.

Over the next few hours, the results continued to come in. When all the votes had been counted, the result was clear. Joe had lost.

'I'm so sorry,' Joe said, at last. 'Jenkins, can you get Theodore on the phone, I should say congratulations. It's the right thing to do. It's important to do the right thing. If only I'd realized that two weeks ago, maybe things would have been different.'

'Theodore Flunk, Sir . . .' Jenkins said, handing Joe the phone.

'Congrat—' Joe started, but he had to hold the receiver away from his ear because there was too much laughter booming down the line.

Theodore yelled down the line, 'Hey Joe, what has two thumbs and the keys to Downing Street? ME!'

'Righto. Well, I just wanted to say well done, I'm sure you're going to make a brilliant Prime Minister . . .' Joe turned to his friend, covering the phone with his hand. 'He's singing "We Are The Champions".'

'What a charmer,' Jenkins said, shaking his head.

'Nope, he's gone,' Joe said, looking at the phone. 'He mentioned something about a conga.'

'Maybe it's not too late to reopen the bow-tie shop,' Jenkins sighed. 'I'm not sure I want to work for someone like him.'

'I would actually like to offer you a job, Jenkins,' said Joe.

'What?' Jenkins asked.

'And you, Ajay. And Alice, too.'

'What's going on?' Joe's mum asked. 'You're not going to start eating jelly again, are you?'

'No, I'm fine, look, I'm happy!' Joe replied.

'I know. That's what I'm worried about, son. You lost, remember?'

'Sure, he lost,' said Alice, turning to Joe. 'So what happens now?'

'At last!' Joe grinned. 'Someone on the same page as me!'

'Sir,' Jenkins said, 'you're not Prime Minister anymore.'

'I know,' Joe said. 'But now I know what I have to do. Now, more than ever, we have to work hard to fight for the things that we care about. I know I lost the election, but that's not the most important thing.'

'What's more important than winning?' Ajay asked.

'Remembering who I am and that the things I believe are really important. If it took something like this to realize, then, as sad as this all is, something good has come out of it. Staying true to your own beliefs and fighting for the things that you care about are bigger than winning or losing elections. So now I know that, the campaigning begins. Yes I lost, but does that mean we should give up on the things like the Green Space initiative? No! We should fight harder.

'It's not going to be easy to pick ourselves up and battle against the likes of Theodore Flunk, but we have to keep going. I want to form a political party, with just kids, to give them their say. I want people to listen to us, and turn our passion into a movement. Alice, I want you to be joint leader with me. I want us to change the world together. You have some brilliant ideas and I think together we could do great things. What do you say? We could work out of my house until we can find an office.

'Ajay, we're going to need some help to spread the word, so just like before, we'll need a camera. No fancy scripts, no focus groups telling me what haircut to have, or what tie goes with which suit, just Alice and I talking to people.

'Jenkins, Alice and I will need your advice, too. I've never set up a political party before, and I need your help with that and well, probably a million other things that I haven't thought of.

'Alice, we need a new way of doing politics, where we can work together instead of just sniping and shouting at each other all the time. I want the grown-ups to stop behaving like sulky kids, and behave more like, well, *real* kids!'

'Mum, I don't know what I need from you, apart from tea and biscuits. We'll work every day after school, once homework is done and probably most weekends, too. I know I'm asking a lot, but I really feel we can do great things if we work together. So who's in?!'

THE END . . . OR IS IT?

What if things had been different? What if Joe hadn't lost?

Joe snapped out of his daydream to the sound of Big Ben chiming ten o'clock.

'Sir, the polls have closed and the results are coming in—good luck!'

Ajay switched on Channel 10 news.

'Hello, here I am, back on terra firma again!' Charlie Jones said, getting out of the heli-telly-studio and kissing the floor. 'I'm alive, ALIVE! Now, to the person who invented this thing, fire them and burn it.'

'It's time for the results! As Big Ben strikes ten and the polls close, we make our first predictions.'

Joe grabbed his mum's hand and Ajay grabbed Jenkins' hand.

'We predict,' said Charlie, 'that it seems to be ... a draw.'

Over the next few hours, the results continued to come in. When all the votes had been counted, the result was clear. It was a dead heat.

'So that's it,' said Charlie James. 'It's a draw. Exactly the same number of votes each! This is incredible! And so, it seems that there's going to be a coalition.'

'A coal addition?' Ajay said.

'No, a coalition,' Jenkins said, correcting him.

'A cold tradition?'

'No, coalition,' Jenkins said again.

'A . . .' Ajay started.

'No, a coalition!'

'Hey, how do you know I was going to get it wrong this time?' Ajay asked.

'Just a hunch,' Jenkins said. 'A COALITION means that there is no clear winner, and that Joe and Theodore must run the government together.'

'Together?' Joe asked.

'Together?' Ajay and Alice said.

'Yep,' Jenkins nodded.

'Right . . .' Joe said, pacing up and down. 'OK, I can do this. It'll be like that day in science when I got lumbered with the really annoying kid. Slowly and surely we worked together, got to know each other, and eventually became friends. Remember, Ajay?'

'I remember! We aced that science project and we've been firm pals ever since,' Ajay nodded.

'So how will it work?' Joe asked.

'I will be the Prime Minister!' Theodore Flunk said, bursting into the room, along with Johnson, his hapless assistant.

'Blimey!' Joe said, taken aback. 'I didn't expect you to arrive here so quickly.'

'Right, bring it in lads!' Theodore said, talking to some removal men. 'Can you put the TV there, and the big chair there, in front of the TV.'

'Erm, I think we need to have a negotiation first,' Jenkins said to Flunk, 'so we can work out the important things, like . . .'

'Where the telly goes?' Flunk said. 'OK, let's have a "negotiation".' Flunk said, doing air quotes with his fingers.

'Well, all right, I am the current Prime Minister, so I should stay on,' Joe started to say.

'NO!'

'Well, OK, what do you think should happen?' Joe asked.

'I'll cut to the chase. Everything that you suggest that starts with "if I stay on as Prime Minister" I'll just yell no to. So let's change tack, what do I have to give you to make you give up the job title?' Theodore asked.

Joe looked at Alice. 'I want a park on every street so kids, well, so anyone, can enjoy green spaces,' Joe said, steeling himself for Flunk's response.

'Please Mr Theodore Flunk,' Alice joined in, 'to have a place to play, sit, you know, just be happy, it would mean so much to me, and every kid I know!'

'Fine, have it, it's yours,' he said. 'But I'm Prime Minister. Is that a deal?'

'Deal,' Joe said, taking a deep breath, knowing in that second, he'd got what he wanted and lost everything at the same time.

'YEEEEES!' Flunk cried, putting his hands over

his head, and doing a knee slide as though he'd scored a goal in the Champions League Final. 'I won. Suck it up losers,' he said putting his finger and thumb on his forehead.

'Errr, I don't want to nitpick,' Ajay said, 'but I think that you're supposed to make the letter 'L' on your forehead, you know, for losers.'

'That's what I'm doing,' Flunk said.

'Well, it's the wrong way round, and upside down. What you've made is a lovely, but altogether useless, number 7,' Ajay shrugged.

'Perhaps we should work out exactly how this is going to work?' Joe suggested, trying to bring the conversation back round.

Flunk ignored Joe, and picked up a picture hanging on Joe's wall. 'What's this? I don't like it.'

'It was a gift from the Indian Prime Minister. It is very expensive and very precious,' Jenkins said, grabbing it off Flunk.

'Yeah, well, I have my own pictures I want to hang up. You, hang my pictures up please!' Flunk said to another removal man.

'Oh my,' Alice's dad said, covering Alice's eyes.

'What is that?' Joe asked, looking at the picture.

'I painted it. It's a self-portrait,' Flunk said. 'It took me ages and it is brilliant.'

'Why are you shirtless?' Ajay asked.

'We're all shirtless beneath our clothes,' Flunk said, straightening the picture now hanging on the wall.

'What are you sitting on?' Alice asked.

'A dragon. I drew a dragon. Dragons are cool.

They're probably the coolest thing in the world,' Flunk said, deadly serious.

'Oh my gosh, he's a moron,' Jenkins whispered to Joe.

'Well, I think your picture is a real smasher,' Joe said enthusiastically.

'Listen, I really think we need to sort out how we're going to make all this work . . .'

'Crown,' Flunk said. 'I want a crown. I've been after this job for so long, now that I have it, I want a crown and maybe a sword too. Do Prime Ministers normally carry a sword? Oh I know, I'll get a lightsabre!'

'Lightsabres aren't real,' Ajay pointed out.

'That's what they said about dragons, but there's one right there,' Flunk said, pointing at his painting.

'Unicorns are waaaay cooler than dragons,' Alice interjected.

'Dragons eat unicorns for breakfast!' Johnson, Flunk's assistant, yelled back.

'OK, so I think we're getting a little off track,' Joe said.

'Oh lighten up!' Flunk sighed. 'Is this table made of chocolate, and can I eat it?'

'No,' Jenkins said, tapping the table. 'It's just a table.'

'I would have thought it would be made of chocolate or something, I mean, this is Downing Street, it's like living in the best mansion in the world. I want the table made of chocolate.'

Joe looked at Theodore incredulously. 'Do you know what being Prime Minister actually involves? Meetings. That's it, all day, every day. Then occasionally I turn up to do Prime Minister's Questions, when you normally shout at me and tell me how terrible I am, then there are more meetings. Sure, I had the stairs replaced with a pole, but that was for efficiency purposes. I don't spend all day, every day eating the furniture and swinging a sword around.'

'BORING!' Flunk said.

'OK, imagine our country as . . . as a giant flying dragon which needs two people to steer it.' Joe said, desperately.

'Ooh, that's better. I'm listening.'

'Well, we both need to work together to find the right direction, steer the dragon away from danger, and stormy weather,' Joe said, looking at Jenkins and shrugging. 'You're at the front, and I'm helping you out.'

'I like the sound of that,' Flunk said to Joe.

'Thanks. Now, I know we've had our differences, but I'd like to help you as best I can. And I would also really like Alice to help, and Ajay and Jenkins too.'

'Yes, yes, yes . . . boring!' Flunk said.

'So . . . that's OK then? You don't mind who I get to help me?' Joe clarified.

'I don't care about parks, I only pretended to care because you liked them so much. To be honest, I don't really care about much. But I did really like what you were saying about the dragon,' Flunk said, getting out a tape measure and looking at the curtains. 'I have some cool Darth Vader curtains that would look good here.'

'Well, OK then. I'll go and find another office,' Joe said.

'Oh look: there's a shed at the bottom of

Downing Street garden, you can work in there. That way, I can keep an eye on you,' Flunk said.

'OK, we can do that. It'll be bracing, working out in nature!' Joe smiled. 'So just to confirm then: you are now Prime Minister and I am second in command. Well, I suppose that concludes things. Congrats again . . . Prime Minister.' Joe felt a twinge of sadness as he said the words, realizing that he wouldn't be running the country alone anymore.

'What about all the stuff we have to do now?' Flunk said, sitting in his new chair and turning the TV on.

'What do you mean?' Joe asked.

'Well, there's loads of things we need to do like running schools, hospitals, the police, and sorting out money and the roads and things. I'll need someone to do all that for me.'

'Would you like me to take care of all that for you?' Joe asked.

'Yes!' Flunk said, nodding. 'Listen, I worked incredibly hard to get here. It's taken me all my life to finally be Prime Minister, and now it's time to relax.

I am quite tired you know, so I intend to do as little work as possible. I need someone to do all the actual work, and I, as Prime Minister, choose you!'

'You want me to do all the jobs while you relax?' Joe said.

'Yep! Oh, and I'd like a cup of tea please, too,' Flunk said.

'Yes, Prime Minister.' Joe couldn't help sharing a smile with his friends. He might have to share power with Theodore, but Joe could still make some great decisions about running the coutry, and the Green Space initiative was first on his list.

'Well, get on with it! I'm parched! Kettles don't just boil themselves and countries don't just run on their own, you know.'

'Yes, Prime Minister,' Joe sighed. He looked over at Jenkins, Ajay, and Alice. 'I think we're gonna need a bigger shed.'

THE END.

WHICH STORY GETS YOUR VOTE?

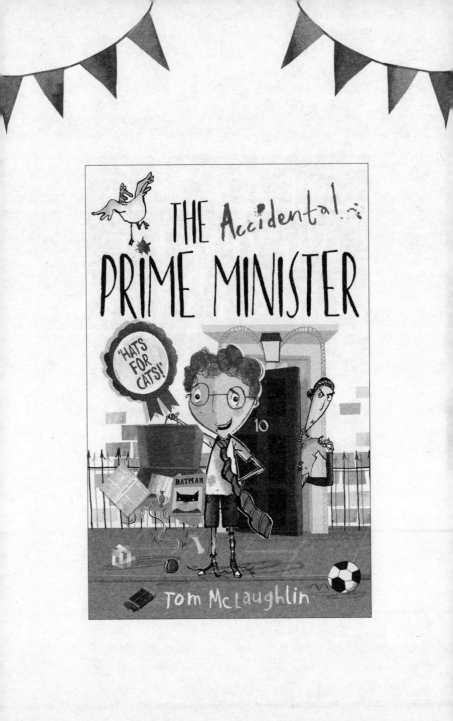

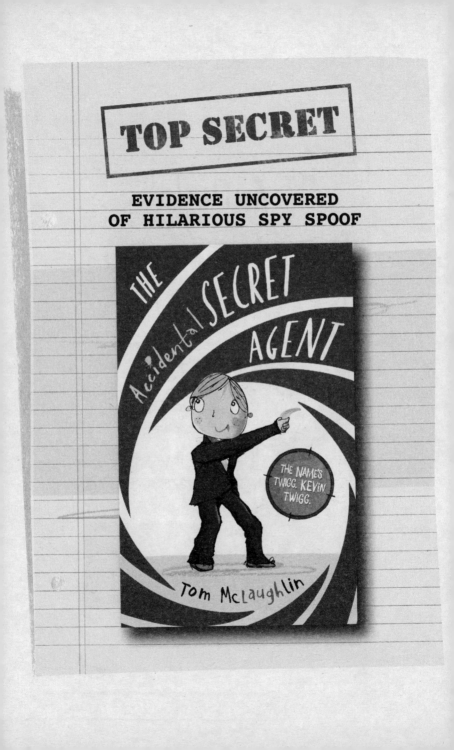

ABOUT THE AUTHOR

Before becoming a writer and illustrator Tom spent nine years working as political cartoonist for *The Western Morning News* thinking up silly jokes about even sillier politicians. Then, in 2004 Tom took the plunge into illustrating and writing his own books. Since then he has written and illustrated picture books as well as working on animated TV shows for Disney and Cartoon Network. *The Accidental Prime Minister Returns'* is the seventh book in his 'Accidental' series.

Tom lives in Devon and his hobbies include drinking tea, looking out of the window, and biscuits. His hates include spiders and running out of tea and biscuits.

CONTINUE THE LAUGHS!